Freedom's Pen

DAUGHTERS OF THE FAITH SERIES

Freedom's Pen

A STORY BASED ON THE LIFE OF FREED
SLAVE AND AUTHOR PHILLIS WHEATLEY

Wendy Lawton

MOODY PUBLISHERS
CHICAGO

All Scripture quotations are taken from the King James Version.

Published in association with the Books & Such Literary Agency, 52 Mission Circle, Suite 122, PMB 170, Santa Rosa, CA 95409-5370, www.booksandsuch.biz.

Editor: Cheryl Dunlop
Interior Design: Ragont Design
Cover Design: Barb Fisher, LeVan Fisher Design
Cover Photos: pen and quill - © christine balderas / istockphoto
          betsy ross flag - © Nic Taylor / istockphoto;
          girl/inset - © Image Source Photography
          poppies - © Aleksej Starostin / shutterstock

Library of Congress Cataloging-in-Publication Data

Lawton, Wendy.
     Freedom's pen : a story based on the life of freed slave and author Phillis Wheatley / Wendy Lawton.
          p. cm. — (Daughters of the faith series)
     Summary: A fictionalized biography of the girl who was brought to America from Gambia as a slave and who later gained fame as an African American poet of great renown, from her time in Africa until she gained her freedom.
     ISBN 978-0-8024-7639-5
     1. Wheatley, Phillis, 1753-1784—Juvenile fiction. [1. Wheatley, Phillis, 1753-1784—Fiction. 2. African Americans—Fiction. 3. Slaves—Fiction. 4. Poets—Fiction. 5. Massachusetts—History—Colonial period, ca. 1600-1775—Fiction.] I. Title.

PZ7.L4425Fr 2009
[Fic]—dc22

2008034333

We hope you enjoy this book from Moody Publishers. Our goal is to provide high-quality, thought-provoking books and products that connect truth to your real needs and challenges. For more information on other books and products written and produced from a biblical perspective, go to www.moodypublishers. com or write to:

Moody Publishers
820 N. LaSalle Boulevard
Chicago, IL 60610

1 3 5 7 9 10 8 6 4 2

Printed in the United States of America

To Emma Berdino,
A Daughter of the Faith

Contents

Under the
Baobab Tree

The Gambia, Africa 1761

She heard it again—that unmistakable *bwaamb, bwaamb* sound. It came from far away, but she was sure it was the *tama*, the talking drum.

Janxa stood still, straining to hear. She waited. Though she could do nothing about the buzz of insects and chattering of monkeys over the wet rice field, she barely breathed. Yes, it was the rhythmic *tama* voice carrying through the forest. The tonal variations sounded like a man talking.

"What do the drums say, *Maamanding*?" Janxa could pick out a few words, but her mother understood the language of the drums. "What are they saying?"

"Hush." Her mother had been bending over the young rice plants all morning, weeding and thinning. She planted her hands on either side of her back and straightened her body up, rubbing circles on her back. Her dress—her *mbubba*—had been tied up between her legs to keep it out of the water as she worked. She reached down to untie it as she continued to listen to the talking drum.

Other women who'd been working the rice fields stopped to listen as well. Janxa could see excitement light their eyes.

"What?" she asked her mother.

"The *tama* is from the village downriver. The *griot* is leaving their village. He will be here before the sun goes to sleep."

The *griot*!

Janxa wrapped her thin arms around herself as if she needed to squeeze in her excitement to keep it from exploding. Janxa had been birthed just before the start of the rains. But now, she had already passed her seventh rainy season. At seven, she was big enough to help her mother in the rice field and to keep her little brothers entertained back in the village. And, at seven, she had seen the *griot* at least that many times. Maybe more. She knew the fathers had been expecting him, but they never knew for sure when he'd arrive. Sometimes he had to stop in a village for a naming ceremony or to sing praises for the visit of an important person.

She had heard that some villages, very big villages, had their own *griots*. What would it be like to have the storyteller in your village every single day? How would you get any work done?

Her mother reached down to pick up her basket. "Come, child, we must go back and prepare food." She called out to the other women as they gathered children and tools. "What will you cook?"

"I have groundnuts to prepare," said one of the young

mothers as she took a length of bright cloth and tied her baby around her chest for the walk back to the village.

The thought of groundnuts made Janxa's stomach rumble. She loved them no matter how they were cooked. She especially liked to eat them fresh.

"I will prepare *couscous*," said Dunxa. "My son supplies me with more millet from his last harvest than I can possibly use."

Janxa smiled. She knew the other women had grown tired of hearing Dunxa brag about her son. Today it wouldn't matter though. The *griot* was coming. Tonight would be a celebration.

As she balanced her mother's tools and hurried to keep up, she couldn't help thinking about the *griot*. She wondered if he'd bring his son.

"Why must the *griot* pass down his calling to his son?" she asked her mother. "What if a new storyteller were to come from another family?"

"It goes from father to son because it is Allah's will," her mother answered.

She should have known. That was the answer to everything. "But what if Allah chose someone else to become a *griot*?"

Her mother didn't answer. She just picked up her pace.

Janxa had to run and hop through the thick elephant grass to keep up. "What if a girl wanted to become a *griot*?"

Her mother stopped walking and turned to look at Janxa, who stopped as well. *Maamanding* spoke no words, but her look told her daughter she had asked one too many questions. "Come, daughter. We have work to do." Her mother turned again toward the village. "Women's work."

When they got to the village her mother went straight to their hut to begin making maize porridge. "Go fetch your brothers home," she said.

As Janxa drew close to the grandmother's hut she saw her little brother, Baaku, playing with sticks on the packed dirt outside the door. The grandmother sat on a bench holding the baby. Baaku ran to Janxa. "Did you hear the *tama*? Did you hear about the *griot*? He's coming."

"I did," she said, laughing at the excitement in her brother's voice. She turned toward the grandmother. "How do you fare today, Grandmother?" The grandmother was not her own grandmother, but everyone called her that out of respect.

"I fare well, Janxa." She jostled the baby to wake him. "I hope this one's not too sleepy to walk."

"I can carry him."

The grandmother made a hooting sound. "You are too thin to carry this one." She squeezed the baby's thigh. "Little Caaman is nearly your size already."

Nothing irritated Janxa more, though she would never let on so as to dishonor the grandmother. She knew she was small, but it didn't mean she couldn't do things. It was true, her brothers were both born plump and sturdy. They had broad features and a rich dark skin. When her mother rubbed palm oil on them they were beautiful. Why did her own build have to be thin and delicate?

"He will walk," she said to the grandmother as she helped Caaman wake. "If they are good, I'll tell them a story while *Maamanding* prepares food."

Both boys clapped their hands. "We love Janxa's stories,"

Baaku said. He began to run ahead but stopped and came back to the grandmother. "Thank you for taking care of us today."

She patted his head before he took off. Janxa and Caaman followed.

"Slow down, Baaku. Caaman cannot keep up with you."

"Can you start the story?" he asked as he slowed his pace.

Janxa took a breath and began to wind out a tale in the soft tones of their Wolof language. Anyone listening closely could catch the rhythm of the talking drum in her telling. The rise and fall of her words conjured up crafty baboons, wise elephants, and no-good hyenas. Her brothers slowed their pace so as not to miss a single word.

The *griot* had been as good as his word. He arrived in the village just as the sun slipped behind the trees. He was welcomed by all the fathers and given the place of honor under the giant baobab tree. The oldest and most honored men sat nearest him, followed by the younger men and then the boys. The women and girls served food, carrying large decorated bowls made from calabash gourds. Even Janxa carried food.

The *griot*'s son sat on the ground near his father's feet. He must have seen about ten or twelve rains. Janxa offered him a maize cake. How fortunate he was to be the son of a great *griot*.

Following the meal everyone stood to stretch. The women cleared the baskets and gourds and carried them to the huts. As soon as they returned, the drummer began to beat out a rhythm on the *tama*. It started slow but rose to a fevered pitch as dancers jumped into a clearing in the center of the swaying people. The *griot* joined the beat of the *tama* with music from his *kora*. Janxa loved watching the explosive movements of the dancers. They'd jump and lift their knees high into the air, colorful *mbubbas* flapping, all while keeping perfect rhythm.

After the dances and the food, everyone settled back to listen to the *griot*. The women sat apart from the men and boys but close enough that they didn't miss a word. Janxa settled herself against a nearby tree to listen.

The village elder began by asking questions about the other places the *griot* and his entourage had visited.

"I will tell you in due time," the *griot* answered, "but first let me sing of your village." He placed his *kora* in front of him and began to pluck the strings and sing.

You offer shelter to the wandering.
Under your tree the wise ones sit and talk.
You feed the children and the ancient ones.
Under your tree the wise ones sit and talk.
Your fields yield rice, juju beans, and millet.
Under your tree the wise ones sit and talk.
You tend to the goats and chase the baboons.
Under your tree the wise ones sit and talk.

He continued to sing praises of their village. Janxa watched his son mouthing the words after his father. Before he could become a *griot* he'd have to learn how to measure a village at a glance and create a song for them without any practice. He'd also have to be able to recite all the history of their people from as far back as anyone could remember.

Once the *griot* finished the praise song, he began to sing songs and tell stories of the great deeds of their people. How did he remember all the names, generation after generation? As her mother stood up to leave, carrying a sleepy Caaman and trailing a reluctant Baaku, Janxa begged to stay. She looked over at her father and he nodded, so her mother let her stay.

She could have listened all night. The *griot*'s stories would stay forever in her memory, mingled with African night sounds—birds fussing as they settled in to roost, the roar of a faraway lion, the eerie laugh of a hyena scavenging for food, and the soft wind rustling the leaves of the baobab.

"After morning prayers," the *griot* said finally as the fire began to die, "I'll tell news of other people and about the great trouble."

No one dishonored him by asking further questions, but Janxa could see that many wanted to hear the news tonight.

She hadn't realized how tired she was, but when her father came over and picked her up to carry her back to her mother's hut she didn't protest. As she snuggled into his arms, she thought, *This is my happy seat—right in the middle of my family.*

Janxa watched her brothers sleep while her mother went out before dawn to draw water. Caaman made little sucking sounds with his lips as he slept. What kind of men would her brothers become? Would they be great hunters like their father?

She sat in the doorway of the hut so she could witness the

beginning of the day and smell the richness of the damp earth before the hot sun began baking it.

Janxa watched her mother coming back with the gourd filled with water. For as long as she could remember, her mother had greeted the sun by raising her gourd high above her head and pouring a drizzle of water out as an offering. She'd then fall to her knees in prayer. Janxa loved watching her mother, straight and tall, lifting water to the sky.

"Come," her mother said as she brought the remaining water to the hut, "let's feed the family and go to the baobab to hear what the *griot* will tell us. Take this bowl to your father. When he has eaten you may go with him, and I'll meet you there."

Janxa took the bowl of porridge to her father's hut and waited quietly while he finished it. She washed the gourd with sand until it was clean.

"Will you go to your mother or come with me?" her father asked.

"May I come with you?"

He smiled at her. "Yes, little one, but you know you cannot sit with me."

She knew that. The fathers were honored and always sat apart. The boys as well. Her father even lived in a hut set apart from theirs—that was the way of her people.

As they drew closer, they could see that the *griot* had already started to sing a song of the morning.

When he finished, they all sat silently, waiting for him to begin.

"The treachery of the *tubaab* grows."

Janxa knew the word *tubaab*. It meant people with no color

—white people. She heard the stories whispered often, but she'd never seen a *tubaab*. She had seen a white baboon once, but never a white man.

"The *tubaab* continues to steal our people. He's now taking more than just the slaves captured in battle."

Janxa knew that when one tribe fought another tribe, they took captives. Her village had not fought in her lifetime, so she didn't know anyone who'd been taken, but the mothers talked about people they once knew who never came back. They believed those captives had been sold to the *tubaab*.

"More often now, *tubaab* has African helpers who ambush warriors caught alone in the bush or young men guarding goats or crops." He stopped and pulled a piece of elephant grass from the ground. "They disappear never to be heard from again."

"What happens to these captives?" the elder asked.

"None have returned to tell. There are some who believe the *tubaab* take our people to eat them."

Janxa's heart beat hard against her chest. *Eat them?* She looked at her father. What would she do if someone took her father? She jumped when she heard the sudden chattering commotion of a group of monkeys far up in the branches of the baobab. Had they seen something? She looked at the faces of the fathers, but no one seemed concerned.

"They've begun taking many more of our people than ever before. We need to be on the lookout for these evil ones." He stopped and put a hand on his son's shoulder. "Even more troubling is that they've been taking children when they can't find men or women."

Children! Janxa looked around for her mother and scooted closer to where she sat with Baaku and Caaman. Who would ever take a child away from family? What kind of people were these *tubaab*?

Song for a Gazelle

The *griot* and his travelers had been in the village for nearly a moon when Lamin died. He'd been older than Janxa—old enough to go out and tend goats. It had been goats that had caused the trouble. Janxa heard her father telling her mother that one of the baby goats had gotten tangled in underbrush and Lamin, without poking the bush with a stick first, reached in to free the kid's leg. A snake bit him.

After one of the boys came to get help, she watched the fathers run to the field where the boys had been grazing the goats. As Lamin's father carried him back, Janxa could see that his arm had already started to swell.

For three days everyone hushed when they neared his mother's hut. Sometimes Janxa could hear his mother crying out. She wondered how long it would take for Lamin to get well.

"Lamin died," her mother told her in a whispery voice that morning. "It is a good thing since the *griot* is still here."

How could it be a good thing that he died? Janxa had seen enough death in her life to know it was *not* a good thing. She remembered the time she'd walked to the rice field with her mother just in time to see a leopard leap from a tree on top of a gazelle calf. Janxa could not look as the cat killed the helpless baby while the gazelle mother watched, frozen in place.

Janxa's mother had hurried her on to the rice field, telling her it was the way of nature, but as Janxa looked back she could see the leopard dragging the lifeless body up into a tree to feed on later.

As she worked beside her mother that day, she composed a praise song for the tiny gazelle.

From your mother's side you walked.
You feared not the predator.
You walked in trust.
You never knew, you never saw, you never felt.
I hold the memory of you forever.

She repeated it to herself, but she didn't dare tell her mother. No one but the *griot* made praise songs. She didn't have a *tama* or a *kora*, but when she was alone, while her mother cooked the meal that night, she upended her calabash bowl and, with a stick, beat out the rhythm of her song.

How she wished she could sing the song for her village. She wondered what it would be like if her song were to be remembered forever, just as she promised to remember the gazelle.

"How is it a good thing that Lamin died?" she asked her mother.

Her mother looked up from grinding the couscous. "What do you mean, a good thing?"

"You said it was a good thing Lamin died because the *griot* is still here."

Her mother made a high-pitched keening sound—almost a wail. "No, no. I only meant that his memory would last from generation to generation because the *griot* will make a song for him. It is not good that he died." Her mother ground the millet harder with her pestle. "But it is the will of Allah," she said, as if only remembering belatedly, "so maybe it is a good thing."

The will of Allah. Janxa had heard those words for as long as she could remember. What did they mean? Most times the words were followed by a shrug of the shoulders. It was almost like when the Harmattan raged—that great wind that blows off the Sahara. When Janxa had only seen two or three rains, she once told her mother, "Make it stop, *Maamanding*." She hated the way the sand got in her eyes and nose. She felt like she was eating dirt the whole time the Harmattan blew.

"It blows, little one," her mother said. "It blows where it pleases and stops when it pleases."

    ❧   ❧   ❧   ❧

Soon after the burial of Lamin, the *griot* took his leave and things settled back to normal in the village. The grandmother cared for the little ones. The mothers tended the rice fields. Dunxa still bragged about her son. The goats were herded to fresh grazing and the fathers hunted. They were moving toward harvest time and much work had to be done.

Janxa spent her days helping her mother or minding her little brothers.

The only darkness that intruded was the increasing talk of *tubaab*. Janxa had learned to recognize the word, so when she heard the drums telling another story of *tubaab* evil, her heart thudded along with the drums. The *griot* had said they even took children.

One day, toward the end of harvest, Janxa followed her mother to her father's hut to help carry food. When they got there, she noticed that her father had his robe tied across his shoulder, ready for travel. He reached out a hand to touch *Maamanding*. Janxa didn't often witness their tenderness, so she turned her head.

"I will go to the Fula," her father said. "I will buy a calf for us."

Her mother smiled. Nearly everyone had goats, but cattle were rare. "The harvest was good?"

"Yes, very good. Allah be praised." He turned toward Janxa. "If I allow you to accompany me, can you walk a long distance?"

"I can. I can." Janxa could hardly believe what her father was suggesting. She looked at her mother. Would her mother let her go?

"Can you carry her if she tires?"

Her father laughed. "She's just a wisp of chaff. Do you think she's too heavy for me?"

Janxa was so excited she could not even take offense. She could see her mother relenting.

"Let me go and pack food for the journey."

They had been walking for much of the day when her father stopped by a stream to rest. He took maize cakes out of his pack and filled their gourds with water from the stream.

Janxa felt too tired to talk.

They had only rested for a short time when her father stood up and walked around their resting place, his eyes on the ground and a worried look on his face. "Come, daughter, be silent," he whispered. "We must leave." He had barely hoisted her onto his hip and slung his bundle across his head when he silently took off, skirting toward the brush.

He continued to move, watching from side to side. Janxa wondered if he'd seen lion tracks or the spoor of some other predator. She knew not to ask. Her father hardly made a breathing sound. As night fell, she listened to the sounds of the nighttime jungle—a faraway roar of a lion, the crashing underbrush caused by some nocturnal hunter. Each noise seemed familiar. Her father's wariness eased.

"Climb down, little daughter. We can rest."

"What did you fear, Father?" Janxa asked.

"I can't be sure. I saw footprints that had no toes. They were made by no animal I recognize. Perhaps they were made by a tool of some kind." His forehead creased. "But they were shaped like a foot."

He gathered her into his lap and wrapped his cloak around both of them. "Sleep, Janxa. I will keep watch."

She didn't know how long she'd slept, but she woke to her father gently shaking her, with a finger placed over her lips. As she shook off the mist of sleep, she heard clumsy movements nearby. Dawn had only begun to streak the sky, so all she could see were dark silhouettes against the lightening sky.

A flock of birds startled and flew up into the trees right beside Janxa, but she managed to stay still and silent. What had startled them?

She soon caught an unfamiliar scent—something cooking? Something burning?

She heard a string of sounds. It was a human voice—she knew that. The words didn't sound like any words she'd ever heard. It wasn't Fula or Mandinka. She felt her father stiffen. She understood what his body told her. Don't move. Don't swallow. Don't breathe.

A deeper voice spoke. It sounded slow and clipped. At the end of one group of sounds, the voice went up, as if the man asked a question. What kind of tribe spoke like that?

Back and forth. There were two men, she could tell by the tone of their voices, but they spoke gibberish. It sounded like a bitten-off tooth language instead of a rich, round language using the throat, the tongue against the roof of the mouth, and lip sounds.

As they moved off, she caught sight of them. They wore strange clothing and their feet looked like hooves of some kind. She caught her breath. *Tubaab!* Their skin . . . they had hair coming out of white faces.

They continued to move off. They hadn't heard the thumping of her heart against her chest. She knew her father had felt it though. His arm had tightened around her.

"We must go back to our village and warn our people," her father said when they were sure the *tubaab* had gone.

Janxa didn't even ask about the calf they planned to buy. It didn't matter anymore. She looked down and saw footprints like the ones her father had seen last night. Now she understood what her father described. The strange hooves of these *tubaab* made the prints.

As they retraced their steps, her father kept them close to the brush. Janxa kept looking up at the trees. The skin on the back of her neck prickled, and she flinched as if a leopard stalked them. Would they reach their village by nightfall? How she longed to snuggle next to *Maamanding* on the sleeping mat and listen to Caaman making suckling sounds and Baaku snoring. She hurried her steps.

High up in the trees a group of quarrelsome monkeys made a ruckus. If the monkeys felt safe playing in the trees, she knew there could be no leopards sleeping there. As long as the monkeys chattered, they were safe. Besides, the sun was high enough that the cats would no longer be hunting.

Father stopped and listened hard. He put his fingers over his mouth to warn her to be quiet. The monkeys fell silent as well.

Snap! She heard the sound of a stick breaking as someone moved through the brush. Her father scooped her up in his arms just as two men stepped out from behind a tree. She couldn't tell the thumping of her heart from the wild beating of her father's, but as the men stepped forward, she could see that they were not *tubaab*. Both of them had color—rich deep color. Relief washed over her. These were her people.

"Brother," the tall man said, "where is your family?" His words sounded strange, as if he came from a different tribe.

"Here and there." Her father tried to shrug his shoulders, but Janxa's arms were wrapped around him and she could feel the tenseness of his back. Something was wrong. Why did Father not tell them everyone was back at the village?

"Call to the other hunters so we can meet them," the other one said, smiling.

"He does not hunt," said the tall one, nodding and squinting his eyes against the sun. "He has no weapons, and he's traveling with a child."

Father tightened his grip on her and shifted the bundle tied across his forehead. "Do you have need of something?"

The men moved closer. As Father stepped back they moved to either side of him. Father gracefully let his bundle slide down his back. He set Janxa down and moved away from her. "Stay back," he whispered.

Janxa nodded. She didn't know what was happening, but she knew her father was wise and strong. She would stay out of the way. Pushing the bundle toward the brush under a tree, she stood next to it.

As the tall man kept talking, the other one rushed her father from the side, swinging a thick stick. Janxa flinched as she heard it hit her father with a thud, but before she could even cry out, her father grabbed the stick, twisting it out of the man's hands, and landed a ferocious blow against the man's head that sent him reeling. The other man dived at Father's knees, throwing him off balance. The man and her father both landed with a thud.

Janxa squeezed her eyes shut. She wanted to cry out to Allah for help, but it seemed so useless. This was probably Allah's will just like everything else she ever asked about. She still found herself crying silently for help.

When she opened her eyes, both men were on top of Father. The tall one was fastening metal bracelets of some kind on his hands.

"No!" she cried out. "What are you doing?" She ran toward her father, but the shorter one kicked her away.

"Do not touch her!" Father screamed, thrashing even more violently. He swung his manacled hands and struck one of the attackers.

"What do we do with the girl?" the shorter man asked as he shifted out of reach of her father. "She's hardly worth the trouble. Look at her—skinny and sickly looking. She won't last a week."

"Just leave her for the hyenas."

Her father pushed the remaining man off and rolled to a kneeling position even though metal bands and chains tied his hands together.

"Watch out. He's a wild man." The taller man rubbed his face where he had been struck by the metal. "This one's dangerous even with shackles. He'll fetch a fine price, but how will we ever get him to the island?"

The island? What do they mean?

Her father kicked out with one leg toward the tall man again. The shorter man reached over and grabbed Janxa, squeezing her. He put his hand across her face. His hand was gritty and smelled like dirt and blood and sweat. Her stomach lurched and she started to gag.

"Do not harm her." Father stood up, hands shackled in front of him. "Let her go back to the village, and I will go with you." His voice took on a pleading tone she'd never heard.

She gagged again.

"Take your hand off her mouth unless you want the contents of her stomach all over you," said the taller man.

The shorter man took his hands off her, and she gasped for breath.

"We're going to let her go back to her village?"

She used the hem of her *mbubba* to wipe her face. How would she find her way back home all by herself? Could she leave her father? What about the *tubaab*?

"No. We will take her with us," said the tall one, nodding to himself. "If she is safe, he has nothing to lose. He will fight to the death. No," he said, smiling, "if we have her, we can control this wild one."

Janxa felt relieved. Whatever happened she did not want to leave her father. When she looked at her father though, she did not recognize him. His bruises had begun to swell, but it was more. His shoulders sagged, and he breathed ragged breaths like an old man.

It was as if he already knew what was going to happen.

Middle
Passage

Atlantic Ocean aboard the schooner Phillis, 1761

Janxa tucked herself into her place on the deck of the ship, between two large wooden crates. When she had first discovered this place she found a tattered piece of carpet wedged partway under one of the crates. She managed to wiggle it out and used it to sit on. When the *tubaab* herded the women and children below, she took it with her. So far, no one had taken it away from her.

She stayed well out of the way between the crates, but she could see most of what happened on deck. She watched. If she lived, she promised herself, she would never speak of the things she saw, the things she heard, and the things she felt.

Never.

When she and her father had been captured she'd had no idea what lay in store for them. But somehow her father knew.

She would never forget that day.

The men had who captured them had taken them to a clearing a day's walk from where they had been caught. It was there she saw *tubaab* again. The *tubaab* used other Wolof, Fula, and Mandinka guards like her father's captors. Janxa kept studying these men who looked just like the men in her village. What kind of man would sell his own people for *tubaab* money?

But it wasn't these bad men who drew her attention. It was the other captured people. All gathered together, they looked like a whole village of sad, frightened people who all spoke different languages.

As Janxa and her father were brought to one of the *tubaab*, he pushed right up to Father and forced his mouth open to look at his teeth just as Father would have done to the calf they had planned to buy. As the *tubaab* poked and prodded, looking him over, Janxa closed her eyes. She would not insult her father's dignity by looking.

"This man could be worth something," the *tubaab* said in her own language. How strange it sounded for a colorless person to be speaking Wolof. "But why did you bring this one?" He pointed to her. "She's not worth the rice we'll have to provide."

Her father stiffened. Janxa could sense him ready to do battle.

"We took her because, through her, we could control him." The tall captor bowed to the *tubaab*, pressing his hands together. "Begging pardon, sir, but this one's the strongest and fittest slave we've yet taken. Our bruises tell the tale." He stepped back a step. "We ask a generous portion for him. You'll make a good increase on him."

The *tubaab* stretched his lips over his teeth. It did not pass for a smile. "We'll pay you the customary amount for him because you've thrust his sickly girl on us as well." He turned his back and walked away.

The men who captured them yanked her father over to the other captives and put metal shackles on his feet. They then strung a rusted chain through the wrist shackles, chaining Father to a long line of men.

No one paid attention to her.

"Let's move the cargo out so we can reach James Island by nightfall," said the man she'd come to hate—the tall one. When some of the chained men refused to move, the guards lashed at them with whips. Janxa stepped back, but the end of one caught her across the face. She felt the welt rising on her face as she watched her father catch the end of the whip over and over.

As the long line began to move, Janxa moved with them. *One foot in front of the other. Don't think. Don't look.* She wondered why no tears came to her eyes. Maybe everything inside her had dried up. If these *tubaab* were planning to eat her, by the time she got to this island she would be one hard, dry piece of meat.

She glanced up at her father and she saw his head nod slowly and his eyes crinkle in that way that meant he was proud of her. She inched closer to him so she could touch his leg for a brief moment.

As she continued to follow, her mind darted here and there. *Maamanding.* She wondered when her mother would know that they were not coming home. How long had they been gone? If they had bought the calf instead of being captured, they might be on their way home by now, but it would be too early to be missed. Perhaps they would already be on the island the *tubaab* talked about before her village knew they were gone?

One foot in front of the other.

She looked at the many people captured. Surely there were too many to be eaten. She'd seen money change hands —it was too much money for food. You could buy several cattle for that price.

There were a few other children. Most were boys about Lamin's age. Several women were chained separately. Most of them wept as they walked. Some had babies in their arms.

She remembered how her village had mourned at the death of Lamin. Would they mourn for Father and her?

The *griot*. Would the *griot* write a praise song for her? She stopped to remove a sharp thorn from between her toes. The whip slashed across her arm.

"Keep up."

Her father screamed at the man wielding the whip, but his protests called down blows onto his own back and all those chained near him. It made Janxa determined to do nothing to bring attention to herself, because it would only bring trouble to her father in the end. No matter what, she would keep pace and remain as invisible as she could.

Praise songs. That's what she had been thinking about. If the *griot* were to write a song to her memory, what would he say? All she could think about was the praise song she had composed for the tiny gazelle killed by the leopard. She mouthed the words:

From your mother's side you walked.
You feared not the predator.
You walked in trust.
You never knew, you never saw, you never felt.
I hold the memory of you forever.

⁂

She had repeated those words over and over as she walked the next two days. Though she had written it for the gazelle, the words became her story as well.

She sensed a slowing down on the afternoon of that second day. As they came to a bend in the river, she saw hundreds of people, all chained like her father. They stood waiting to board small boats to take them to the island in the Gambia River called James Island.

For a brief moment, Janxa looked at some of the faces of the captives, but what she saw there reminded her—don't look. One woman reached down to scoop up dirt and hold it close to her chest. The action brought the whip down on her back, but several others did the same. She could hear murmurs in many tribal tongues, but she could pick out the word *home* and the word *Africa* in her own Wolof. They were gathering what they thought might be the last bit of homeland.

The tear of sorrow falls from every eye
Groans answer groans and sighs to sighs . . .

She mouthed the words in her soft Wolof tongue before she stopped herself. No one should make a song of this moment.

She knew that she'd never forget the soft sound of shuffling feet on dirt and the clank of rusty chains being pulled through shackle loops. Her father and the men chained with him climbed into a crowded boat to be rowed to the island. Father watched her, and she never took her eyes off him. She saw him get out of the boat when they landed on the island and disappear into a large hut made of stone.

She shivered and wrapped her arms around herself. She had never been without family before.

But all that had happened more than a moon ago. Now as she sat on this large canoe—this canoe they called a ship—wedged between the wooden crates, she wondered if she had somehow known then. Did she have a sense that she'd not see her father again?

She had been taken to a building with women and children —all mourning their families and their villages.

"I never thought I'd be captured as a slave," said one Mandinka woman.

"Are we all slaves?" Janxa asked.

"Yes, child. Every last one of us."

Sometimes she saw groups of slaves being moved from one place to another on the island. She always searched for a glimpse of her father but never saw him.

She didn't want to remember most of what happened, like the pain of having a hot iron brand the flesh on her back. The burn hurt for days. She looked at the design burned onto the backs of her fellow slaves. Each bore the same marks. One woman said it was the name of their owner.

Janxa hated the brand. It was another sign that she could never go home again. But she kept thinking about what the woman said. Those marks represented a name. She didn't know you could make marks that could represent a name. She never wanted to brand anyone—ever—but she knew she wanted to know the mark that represented her name.

After several days she was taken with a small group of women and children, put in a rowboat, and rowed out to a ship they called a schooner in *tubaab* language. She hoped her father would follow.

"Janxa, are you there?" She heard the whisper of her friend, Obour, and it brought her back to the present. The rocking motion of the boat and her ever-present nausea reminded her if nothing else.

"Shhh. Yes. Come sit with me."

Janxa had met Obour on the island. They'd sat next to each other as they waited. They didn't know what they waited for, but they knew that they were all waiting. The women and children were crowded into a small, hot, filthy-smelling building. Insects buzzed around them. Once a day two men came with an iron kettle of porridge. They offered no gourds. The people just put out their hands, and the men plopped the food into them. Janxa didn't want to remember those days of waiting either.

But now they waited no longer—they were both on this ship, leaving their homeland far behind. Obour squeezed in between the crates next to Janxa. The ship rocked on the waves. It moved up, seemed to pause, and then sank down. Several of the slaves down below were sick. It seemed that the more the ship heaved on the water, the sicker people became. It didn't help that the grain they were given to eat was usually boiled down to a sickly paste. The food was worse than the porridge they'd been served on the island. The *tubaab* who did the cooking didn't even bother to remove the weevils and worms before they cooked it.

Janxa and Obour stayed up on what the *tubaab* called "deck" as much as they could. They had learned that no one paid much attention to children on the boat. The *tubaab* worried most about the men—they seemed to fear them.

"They are bringing out the slaves to dance," Obour said, pulling on her ear. Janxa had noticed that Obour pulled on her ear whenever she worried. "Are you still hoping to see your father?"

"No," Janxa said, wrapping her arms tightly around her body. "If he were on the ship I would have seen him by now. We've watched the fathers brought up from the belly of the ship. We've seen all of them many times but never my father."

At first, Janxa did not understand why these *tubaab* did any of the things they did. Why were all the men chained to long wooden pallets deep in the belly of the ship, stacked one shelf of men on top of the other? There was not even enough room for the fathers to sit—they could only lie on their wooden pallets, day after day. The women and children were not chained. They were crammed into another space, but during the day some of them were allowed up on deck.

The smells deep inside the ship were so awful that they were another reason Janxa spent every moment she could up in the fresh air of the deck. That meant that she was often slapped or kicked or sent down into the hold, but if she stayed out of the way, they often didn't notice her.

"Do you think my father could have escaped and gone back to our village?" Janxa had never voiced the hope out loud.

Obour thought for a long time. In the time Janxa had come to know Obour, she learned that her friend never spoke without giving a matter careful thought. "Before we were taken captive I heard that none had ever escaped from the *tubaab* to come back to tell why the *tubaab* were taking captives."

"I heard the same," Janxa said.

"Do you think he could do what no others have yet done?"

Janxa thought about her father. "Maybe."

"But you've told me many stories about your father. How he fought for you, even when it cost him great pain." Obour measured her words. "I do not believe your father would have escaped and left you in the fort at James Island."

Janxa hated to hear her friend's reasoning, but she heard the truth in them. "You are right, Obour. My father would not have escaped unless he could have taken me with him."

"We know we are sailing to a place called . . . how do they say it? America? Boston?" Obour said the words, trying to mimic what they'd heard in the *tubaab* tongue. "We know there are many ships carrying slaves."

"Yes. We've heard the *tubaab* who speaks Wolof say it to some of the mothers."

Janxa did not want to think about the mothers and what they endured on the ship. She repeated her chant—*don't think, don't look, don't feel.* She had put her head between her knees yesterday when one of the *tubaab* sailors had grabbed a sick baby right out of his mother's arms and thrown the tiny boy into the sea. While the mother rocked and keened throughout the night, Janxa put her fingers in her ears and made a praise song to the tiny baby. As night wore on and sleep wouldn't come, Janxa kept forgetting what the baby had looked like and kept remembering Cáaman instead.

"I think your father may be on another ship to America."

Janxa hadn't considered that. What if they were to find each other? Would they ever be together again? She didn't want to say it out loud to her friend because Obour's mother had died on the island. It didn't seem fair that Janxa could have the hope of seeing a father again when Obour had no hope at all. At least *Maamanding*, Baaku, and Caaman were safe in their village.

She heard the clank of chains and knew the dancing ritual would begin. She hated watching the humiliation of the fathers, so she turned to Obour. "Do you see these marks here?" She pointed to markings on the wooden crates. "I think they are marks that represent sounds or words."

"I don't understand," Obour said. But she was distracted as she stared at the thin men stumbling out of the hold. "Why don't they unchain them? Why don't they give them clothing?"

"Don't look," Janxa said.

Some of the *tubaab* began throwing water on the men and scrubbing them with long-handled brushes.

Though Janxa tried not to look, she knew that the men were chained night and day to their platform except for when they were marched above deck for what the *tubaab* called exercise. It was no way for humans to live. Chained to a ship, a man could not go into the bush to take care of bodily functions. He could not bathe or keep clean here. The belly of the ship reeked with filth and vomit.

Each day the *tubaab* would make the men come up on deck and dance to soulless music played on a *tubaab* instrument. The men didn't dance like they danced in their villages —there was no joy, just a shuffling movement. The mothers said the *tubaab* only did this so the men wouldn't die before the ship arrived in Boston. If they didn't move to the *tubaab*'s liking, the whip slashed through the air and onto their backs until they danced with vigor.

While the men danced, some of the younger *tubaab* tied cloths around their faces and went down into the ship's belly with hot water and something they called vinegar and scrubbed at the filth. It didn't seem to make a difference—the misery and the smell just got worse with each day.

Janxa could only keep herself going if she didn't think too much about it. Instead she watched the *tubaab*. One of them made marks on a thin white skin. She heard him call it a paper. He made the marks with the feather of a bird and some kind of dye. She kept watching the marks and listening to the scratch of the quill. She watched hard and tried to copy the marks in her mind. Once in a while she noticed that he made the same marks as those on the box next to her. She put her finger on her piece of carpet and pretended it was a quill. As he made the marks, she mimicked them. Over and over. She began to see patterns in the marks. That's when she began to suspect that the marks had some purpose.

Once, she saw him go from slave to slave—looking at the person and then making a mark on his paper for each one. She heard him call it writing. That's when she began to understand that those marks represented words spoken or names of people. She fingered the brand burned into her shoulder. The marks on that paper were like her brand. She didn't think anyone from her village knew writing. Did the *griot*? No, he had to remember all the stories of their people so he could speak them.

What if she could learn writing? If she couldn't be a *griot* and have her songs sung, could her words be marked in this writing and remembered forever?

"Come, Janxa." Obour's voice snapped her out of her daydream. "Quickly, down into our place below."

Janxa followed, not knowing why. The smell of filth and vinegar made her stomach lurch. The ship had begun to roll even more violently. "What's wrong?"

"So many have become sick. They are bringing men up from the lowest part of the ship's belly and— You don't want to know, do you?"

"No," Janxa said. Obour was right. She did not want to know, but she wasn't able to stay as blind as she pretended. She knew the *tubaab* would be throwing the sickest slaves overboard to keep the rest from sickening. Obour didn't want her to have to watch.

Janxa left Obour with the other women and squeezed into a far corner, pulling her carpet close to her. She took a small piece of burnt wood she'd found up on deck and scratched one group of marks she had seen on the box—P H I L L I S.

4
Nothing but Chattel

I . . . can't . . . breathe." Janxa gasped the words out. It felt like a great weight on her chest—as though someone squeezed the very breath out of her. She had been down below in their tiny space, and the air seemed to get hotter and heavier as the day wore on.

Obour rushed to get Faja, one of the Wolof mothers. "Should we take her up on deck to get some fresh air?" Obour asked.

"No," said Faja. "If the *tubaab* believe she is sick they may throw her overboard." The mother began pushing everyone away. "Squeeze back as tightly as you can to give the girl room to breathe."

Janxa panicked. She couldn't find her next breath.

"Relax, child," Faja said. "Think of something back in your village to make your body relax enough to let the air in."

Janxa thought hard about *Maamanding* grinding millet. She tried to remember the sound the grinding made. When the panic of not getting any air started to overtake her again, she mouthed the song her mother sang as she worked her pestle. Little by little she felt the tight grip ease, and she could pull a little air into her lungs.

"Hush, everyone," Faja said. "Hush." She began to hum a song *Maamanding* used to hum to the babies.

Janxa pulled some air in through her nose instead of gasping for air through her mouth. The panic eased a little.

Breathe in. Breathe out.

Janxa began to take notice of those around her. All the women and children had pushed as far back against the wall as they could to give her air. She still didn't have enough breath to talk, but she longed to thank them. She knew it was hot and fetid there in the cramped hold. It must have been unbearable to sit and stand pressed tightly against each other. One of the older women knelt, praying. At first Janxa thought she was praying to Allah, but she kept saying the name Yeesu. Janxa wondered who Yeesu was—she'd never heard of a god by that name.

"Are you better, Janxa?" Obour kneeled next to her and held her hand.

Janxa nodded. The other women and children eased forward a little. The rocking of the boat and the soft hum of Faja's song eased the rest of the tightness.

Pretty soon the women and children settled themselves back around Janxa. She pulled her tattered piece of carpet toward the wall and lay down on it. She felt tired but safe.

The days continued one like the other. Their sleeping space grew less crowded as the ship continued across the water. Janxa did not like to think about why. She missed many of the faces that had become familiar. There had been too many losses.

"Obour, do you dream about your village?" she asked as they sat above deck, between the crates. She often dreamed about her father, mother, and brothers. She even dreamed about the *griot*. When she woke to the rocking of the ship and the cries of the other slaves, she missed her family and her village all the more.

"Almost every night. I sometimes even smell the smells of Africa."

"Is your dream more real than this?"

Her friend stayed silent while she thought, but Janxa had become used to that. Finally Obour said, "I think it is. The music is more real, the colors are brighter, the people are more alive." She paused. "I think it is."

"What if this were just a nightmare and our dreams are real?"

"I couldn't dream things this evil. I didn't know about *tubaab* and I could never have imagined the cruelty." Obour pulled on her ear. "No one in my village did the things we've witnessed."

Janxa pressed her hand against her mouth. She'd been worried about her teeth. The two front ones had become loose. As she tested them with her finger and felt them wobble, one came out in her hand. "Oh no!"

"What?" Obour said.

"My tooth just fell out." Janxa almost never cried, but she

couldn't help herself. Was she going to lose one piece of herself at a time?

"Don't cry. Those are just your milk teeth. Everyone loses them."

"They do?"

"Yes. I lost mine about two rains ago."

"But you have all your teeth." Janxa had seen that slow smile enough to know.

Obour laughed. "I have my adult teeth. I had to lose the baby ones in order to get these."

What would she do without Obour? "Will you stay with me wherever we go?"

Obour didn't answer for a long time. When she finally spoke, her voice was far from steady. "I still do not know what will happen to us. Faja understands some *tubaab* language. She said they talk about selling the cargo in Boston. She says we are the cargo."

"You and me?"

"No, all us who are not *tubaab*. I think we will be sold as slaves when we get to Boston."

Slaves. Janxa had never heard of children who were slaves. "If we are sold I hope we will be sold to the same village."

Obour didn't answer.

❧   ❧   ❧   ❧

More than two moons had passed on the sea voyage when Obour shook Janxa awake. "Come, look!"

Janxa followed her friend up to the deck. The *tubaab* seemed distracted and excited. There, off in the distance,

Janxa could see land. How she wished the land could have been Africa, but she knew it was the land they called America. They would be landing at the village of Boston.

"Look at all the other ships," Obour said. "I wonder if your father is on one of them."

Janxa looked hard. She never thought of that. Yes, there were all manner of floating canoes on the water—some much larger than the one she stood on. "Stay with me, Obour," she said as she clutched her piece of carpet.

From that moment on, nothing was the same. The *tubaab* ordered the slaves up on the deck and then back into the ship's belly, scrubbing and whipping and fussing all the time. The women and children were scrubbed and shouted at as well.

All the while, Janxa and Obour clung to each other.

"Whatever you do, stay with me," Obour said. "We don't want to be separated."

Janxa held on to Obour with one hand, and the other clutched her piece of carpet. They tucked themselves between their crates to stay out of the chaos on deck. The *tubaab* chief shouted orders at all the other *tubaab*. Some were climbing the tall trunks that held the flapping cloths. Others tied and untied ropes, wound things up, and reeled things out. Everywhere shouts rang out and feet pounded from one end to the other. Soon the ship was turning, heading toward land.

The girls stood now, hanging on to the rail. It was like nothing Janxa had ever seen. As they came closer to land she understood that Boston was nothing like an African village. They climbed down below where all the other women and children had gone.

No one spoke. The ship had been like a nightmare to all

of them, but Janxa could tell from the faces that it was at least familiar to them. Fear of the unknown etched all of their faces.

The ship bumped something, and several women who'd been standing stumbled against the wall. After so long a time of movement, the ship stood still. It continued to rock on the waves, but it no longer moved through the water.

Mixed with the shouts of *tubaab* on deck, Janxa could hear other sounds. She longed to go up on deck but didn't dare. They heard the sounds of chains running through metal shackles as the men were being brought above deck. After what seemed like a long time, they were directed to go above deck as well.

"Stay with me," Janxa whispered.

"I'm here," Obour said, tightening her grip.

The men looked sick—as if there was nothing but skin stretched over their bones. Janxa looked down at her arms. They were probably smaller than they had been when she left Africa. The trip had been hard and the food scarce. It had taken a toll.

The ship had been tied to the wooden platform on the shore with ropes. A plank had been fixed from the ship to the platform. She heard the *tubaab* calling the platform a dock. After some new *tubaab* came up the plank to talk to the chief of the ship, they lined the men up and had them walk down the plank onto the dock. It wasn't easy. Many of the men were weak and wobbly. She kept watching and squeezing Obour's hand. If just one of the men fell off the plank, all the men chained to him would follow.

It took a long time for the men to leave. Janxa saw the *tubaab* with the writing quill, making marks on his paper.

Finally it was time for the women and children. Janxa was surprised to find herself wobbly as well. Even when she stepped on land, she felt like she was still on a rolling ship. Did this Boston pitch and roll like a ship?

The sounds and smells nearly stopped her. People shouted out things in *tubaab* language. Carts pulled by horses rumbled in the street. She had seen a *tubaab* riding a horse when they walked with all the captives in Africa, but here horses were everywhere. She saw crates of chickens and other animals she didn't recognize. And baskets piled with fish. She saw sacks of maize and rice piled on the dock.

Bur everywhere she looked, she saw writing. As she and Obour followed the women, she saw it marked on the sacks of grain, on pieces of paper fixed to the sides of their huts and walls. She saw a stack of papers with so much writing it looked like ants pouring out of an anthill onto the paper.

"I want to learn writing," Janxa said aloud.

"What's writing?" Obour said. "Are you already talking *tubaab* talk?"

Janxa turned around to take one last look at the ship that took her from Africa. All the people on the dock near the ship covered their faces with cloths. The people of Boston didn't seem to like the smell of the ship any more than the slaves had.

As Obour pulled her, urging her to catch up, something caught her eye. There on the side of the ship was writing. P H I L L I S, it said. The same writing as Janxa had noticed on her crates. Could it be the name of the ship? Maybe the *tubaab* put the writing on the crates to match it to the writing on the ship. Then they could get the right crates to the right ship. What a useful thing, this writing.

"Yes," Janxa whispered, "I want to learn writing."

5
The Print
of His Shoe

Boston, Massachusetts, July 1761

How long do you think we'll stay in this place?" Janxa asked. She looked around the stone building. It was within sight of the slave ship that brought them from Africa. It reminded her of the holding place on James Island.

"I do not know," Obour answered, pulling on her ear. "Each day they take a group of us out of here."

"Where do you think they take them?" Janxa still sometimes worried about the rumors they'd always heard back in Africa.

"Do you not know where they go?" One of the men who could speak both *tubaab* and Wolof spoke. He'd been brought in two days ago and explained that he was a slave who had displeased his master.

"No," Obour said.

The man pointed at a paper with writing on it. "It says

here that an auctioneer, John Avery, is selling us. Says we're a parcel of likely Negroes."

"You can make out that writing?" Janxa moved closer to where the man was shackled by his feet to the wall. She touched the paper. "I want to learn writing."

"You mean you want to read." The man said the word in *tubaab.*

"Read." Janxa repeated the word. "Now I can speak *tubaab.*" She couldn't help smiling, even though she knew she was missing her two front teeth.

He laughed. "The language is English, not *tubaab.* The word *tubaab* is the Wolof word for white men."

"English," Janxa said. "Read English writing."

"Now those are the kind of words that can land a slave in trouble," he said. "Maybe not so much in Boston as down South. If you want to learn to read, you better pray you stay in Boston or points north. Otherwise you don't stand a chance."

"How did you learn to read English writing?" Janxa loved the way the words sounded. The more she said them, the more Obour pulled on her ear, worrying.

"My first master owned a mercantile and wanted me to help him keep accounts, so he taught me to read." He stretched his arms over his head and leaned back, lacing his fingers behind his neck. "He was happy I learned to read business papers and keep track of his accounts. He wasn't so happy when I discovered books."

"So people buy slaves to help them work?" Obour asked, changing the subject. Many of the other Wolof-speaking slaves leaned in to listen.

"Yes. Here in Boston most slaves help in the houses, some in the businesses. Outside the city and down South slaves are needed for field work."

"So what are books?" Janxa asked, ignoring the talk of slaves and work.

The man reached behind him and pulled something out of his waistband. "Come closer," he said. "This is a book." He opened the skin covers, and it bloomed like a flower. "There is writing on every leaf."

Janxa put out her finger and touched a page. No wonder he called the writing papers "leaves"—they looked like delicate dried leaves. "Can you read the English writing?"

He opened it to a page that fell open easily, and in a deep, resonant voice read, "The waters, indeed, are to the palate bitter, and to the stomach cold; yet the thoughts of what I am going to, and of the conduct that waits for me on the other side, doth lie as a glowing coal at my heart." He stopped.

Janxa stood silent for a moment. "Please read a little more."

He smiled and read, "I see myself now at the end of my journey; my toilsome days are ended. I am going now to see that head that was crowned with thorns, and that face that was spit upon for me. I have formerly lived by hearsay and faith; but now I go where I shall live by sight, and shall be with him in whose company I delight myself. I have loved to hear my Lord spoken of; and wherever I have seen the print of his shoe in the earth, there I have coveted to set my foot too."

"You must be a *griot*. I do not understand those English words, but that song is beautiful." Janxa pressed her hands against her chest. "It calls up a longing deep inside."

He laughed. "I'm not a *griot*. They just call me Preacher. The words come from Mr. Bunyan."

"Who is Mr. Bunyan?" Janxa asked.

"He's the man who wrote this book. The name of the book is *Pilgrim's Progress*."

"Books have names?" Obour asked.

"Yes. There are many books, so, like people, they must have names so we can recognize them." He closed the book, ran his hand across the cover, and tucked it back in his waistband.

"I want to read Mr. Bunyan's *Pilgrim's Progress* someday," Janxa said.

The man people called Preacher laughed again. "I think you will, little one. I think you will read and write."

Janxa put her piece of carpet on the floor and sat down. She took her finger and made marks in the dust. P H I L L I S. "What does this say?" she asked.

"It is a woman's name, Phillis." Preacher said the word by brushing his teeth on his lower lip. It sounded soft to Janxa.

"Phillis," she repeated.

"The name sounds too soft and gentle for the name of the slave ship that brought us to Boston," Obour said.

"You came on the *Phillis*?" he asked. "It's not as bad as some. I helped unload it once. It's not a tight pack—that's a ship that packs double the slaves in the same space."

Obour gave him a look of disbelief.

"I know the middle passage. I came to America when I was about your age. It's always filled with horror and loss. It doesn't change no matter how tight they pack it, but the death toll is heavier on a tight pack."

Janxa stopped listening, picked up her carpet, and moved to the other side of the room.

"What's the matter with your friend?" Preacher asked Obour.

Janxa saw Obour hesitate before answering. "She doesn't want to remember."

Preacher had been right. They were to be sold, and John Avery, the auctioneer, did the selling. On a warm morning, Janxa, Obour, three men, and two women were taken out of the room in which they'd been waiting.

Two English-speaking slaves came and rubbed them with oil, just like *Maamanding* used to rub the little boys with palm oil. The oil here did not smell like palm oil, though. The man called John Avery lined all of them up on a platform. All around them people talked *tubaab*. No, Janxa corrected herself—it was English they spoke. Much of the talk was loud and rude. John Avery kept pointing and poking and speaking fast. Sometimes people asked to see inside one of the slaves' mouths and to run hands down their arms and backs. Janxa turned her head so she wouldn't see.

The men sold first. Janxa closed her eyes after she saw the first man unshackled from the others and led away with a rope like a goat.

"Stay with me, Obour," Janxa whispered. Her chest heaved as she tried to breathe.

"Don't do this now, Janxa." Fear colored Obour's voice. "Relax. Remember what Faja said. Think about home."

Janxa took her piece of carpet and pressed it to her chest. *Think about home, about Africa.* She remembered the excitement caused by the arrival of the *griot* and his stories. *Breathe slowly.* She remembered longing to create praise songs herself—how she wanted to become a *griot.* She tried to mouth the words to the praise song she had written:

From your mother's side you walked.
You feared not the predator.
You walked in trust.
You never knew, you never saw, you never felt.
I hold the memory of you forever.

She repeated the words over and over in her mind and slowly her breath returned.

She saw a well-dressed woman pull on her man's sleeve and point to Janxa. Her breath caught again. She pulled her carpet closer to her body to cover herself. *Don't do this. Be strong. Breathe.*

The man asked a question in English, and the auctioneer answered. It went back and forth. The auctioneer called the man John Wheatley.

Janxa tightened her grip on Obour's hand.

After much talk, John Wheatley took a pouch out of his clothing and handed silver coins to the auctioneer, who pushed Janxa toward the man. Since Janxa would not let go of her friend, Obour trailed behind her.

The auctioneer yelled something at Obour and yanked her away, pulling Janxa off balance. Another man came forward with money. He must have asked the price for Obour, because he ended up handing coins to the auctioneer for Obour.

The two girls stood close together as Janxa's new master, John Wheatley, greeted Obour's master.

"They are friends," Obour whispered as she squeezed Janxa's hand. "We will not have to say good-bye forever."

"You must learn to read English," Janxa said as Obour's master began moving away. "I will send you writing."

Janxa watched her friend walk down the dock until she couldn't see her any longer.

•᷍᷍•   •᷍᷍•   •᷍᷍•   •᷍᷍•

The woman, her new master's wife, wrapped a shawl around Janxa and helped her get into the cart they called a carriage. Janxa could feel kindness in her touch. It confused her. This was not how slaves were treated in Africa or on the ship.

Everything was strange—the way the woman smelled, the feel of the carriage, the people—everything.

The woman spoke to John Wheatley and then to Janxa. Janxa couldn't understand what she said. How would she know what to do until she learned English? The woman repeated the question more slowly and a little louder. Janxa heard a familiar word—name. The *tubaab* who did the writing on the ship used this word when he was making marks for each slave.

Janxa smiled. "Name," she repeated.

The woman knitted her brows together, and then her face eased. She put her hand on her chest. "Mrs. Wheatley," she said.

Janxa understood. This woman was Mrs. Wheatley. Janxa pointed her hand toward the woman. "Mrs. Wheatley," she repeated. "Missus" sounded so soft, just like this woman.

The woman said something else to the man and then looked back at the dock where the ship was still tied. She smiled and pointed to Janxa. "Phillis," she said.

Janxa looked back at the slave ship and shuddered. She could smell the stench of it from this distance. Naming had been so important among her people. It made sense to have a new name for a new life—but Phillis?

She put her finger down on the seat beside her and traced the name Phillis, starting with the first mark P and tracing until the last mark. "Phillis," she said and put her hand on her chest.

Mrs. Wheatley's eyes opened wide. She said something to John Wheatley, and he stepped down from his seat and came back to where Janxa sat.

She tapped her finger on the seat where Janxa had made the mark and said, "Phillis."

Janxa traced the marks again and said "Phillis."

John Wheatley stood silent for a moment before he began talking to Mrs. Wheatley. He climbed back up on his seat, and the driver flicked the reins and started the carriage moving.

Janxa considered her new name. Instead of thinking about the ship, she would think about writing every time she heard her new name. She longed to learn writing and to learn to read all the writing in Boston. She wanted to read a book. She wanted to read Mr. Bunyan's *Pilgrim's Progress*.

In this America she was Phillis. She reached her hand down to make sure her piece of carpet was still beside her.

While she lived in Boston, she would not think of herself as Janxa again. She would save that name for her family—for Africa. Maybe someday she would find her father or see her mother and brothers again. Then she would be Janxa. She wondered if the *griot* had already made a song for Janxa. She might never know.

But she didn't think there were any *griots* in America. If Phillis were to be remembered, she'd have to make the song herself. Maybe she could make the song with writing.

6
Neither
Fish nor Fowl

Boston, 1762

Phillis had lived with the Wheatleys for more than a year when the Tanners, Obour's master and his family, came to visit from Newport. Phillis had been looking forward to the day for more than a fortnight. The Tanners had arrived late the night before. They brought some of their own slaves to help with the work. Obour was one of them.

Phillis hadn't dared go to sleep that night. She knew it would take time for the Tanner party to make their way to Boston on a schooner and then pack everyone in hired carriages for the ride to the Wheatley house.

The candle in Phillis's room had burned low by the time she heard a knock at her attic door. The Wheatley housekeeper, Lucy, opened the door and said, "The missus says this girl is to sleep in your room."

Obour walked in, dropped her bundle on the floor, and

ran to hug her friend. Both girls talked at once. Lucy looked at the two of them, put a hand on her hip in disgust, and left the room. She closed the door a little too loudly.

"You have a room to yourself with a fire and candles?" Obour walked around the room touching everything. "I can't believe my eyes."

Phillis understood the unspoken comparison—from the wretched slave ship to the Wheatley mansion. Sometimes she had to pinch herself as well.

They talked until they could no longer keep their eyes open. By the time they crawled into bed, they still had more questions for each other.

"Don't you need to go help the cook or help prepare the dining room?" Obour paced. They'd had breakfast brought up to them on a tray that morning by a sulky Lucy. Obour carried the tray down to the kitchen and tied an apron around her waist. The cooks were out picking fresh vegetables in the kitchen garden.

"No," Phillis said. "I don't have many household duties."

"What do you do all day long?"

"Mary Wheatley tutors me, and I study."

"That is strange." Obour shook her head.

"I know. Sadie, our cook, keeps saying, 'It's just not fitting.'" Phillis wagged her finger, mimicking the cook. "I've given up trying to figure out what is and is not fitting. When I first came here, I didn't understand a thing. And it wasn't just the language—the ways were so different."

"I know," Obour said. "Wasn't it hard trying to work out what we were supposed to do when you couldn't understand a single word of English?"

"Everything seemed so strange. It was another world. Can you imagine what I thought when the carriage pulled up to this house?"

In Africa, Phillis had seen only huts and the stone holding cells of James Island. When they had walked down the plank at the Beach Street Wharf in Boston, she had seen her first brick building. But to have the carriage pull up at the portico of one of the finest mansions in Boston . . . well, it left her stunned. Phillis found she had trouble catching her breath again. She ended up gasping for air.

She didn't understand the words then, but now she understood that Mrs. Wheatley was worried about her breathing. She remembered one word, *asthma*.

Mr. Wheatley had lifted her out of the carriage and deposited her in the kitchen. She had heard Sadie tell the story enough times that she now knew it by heart, but at that moment, she didn't know who these people were or what they planned to do with her.

When she caught enough breath to look around, she saw the huge kettle hanging from the open fireplace. It was big enough for her to fit inside without so much as a toe hanging out. She didn't want to remember what so many in her village thought—that the *tubaab* captured people to eat them.

Even as breathless and confused as she was that day, she knew she hadn't been purchased for food. Preacher, from the holding cell on the Boston wharf, had told them that slaves were bought to work. Besides, she couldn't forget the kindness of Mrs. Wheatley—how she draped a shawl around her to cover her near nakedness and how gently she treated her.

"Are you daydreaming again?" Obour asked.

"I'm thinking of the day I arrived. I was still having a bit of trouble breathing."

"Does that continue to plague you?"

"Yes. Mrs. Wheatley's doctor says it is the asthma. He says I will always have it, especially in this damp climate. I probably had it in Africa, but he says the dry season would have been perfect for keeping my lungs dry."

"Do you suffer much?"

"I seem to be sick all too often, but I can usually keep the spells from getting as severe as the ones you helped me through. Faja was right. Fear tightens everything. I have to stay calm. Do you remember Faja from the ship?"

"I do. And I remember the woman who knelt and prayed to Yeesu during your worst attack. Do you remember her?"

"Yes. As she began to pray, I felt a calmness sweep over me like the wind over the deck of the ship."

"You know now who she was praying to, don't you?"

Phillis hadn't thought about it.

"She was praying to Jesus. *Yeesu* is his Wolof name."

Phillis thought back to that day. Strange. She never connected that prayer to all that she'd been learning here in Boston.

"Have you heard about Jesus?" Obour folded her hands across her apron, quietly waiting for an answer.

Phillis could tell from Obour's seriousness, this was a question she'd been waiting to ask her friend. Phillis smiled. "I spend every day with Jesus now."

Her friend looked puzzled. "No, I mean Jesus Christ, the Son of God, the Most High."

"I was jesting, Obour. Yes, I do know Jesus. I've been reading and studying His Word every single day."

"You read now?" Obour grabbed Phillis's hands. "I am so glad for you. Ever since you discovered writing, that was all you ever wanted to do."

"I know. We've been here sixteen moons—I mean, months—and I can read the hardest passages in the Bible."

Obour wrinkled her nose. "Are you certain? The Bible is very difficult, and you are about two years younger than me."

"I'm not saying I understand everything, but the reading comes very easily to me. Mary has been tutoring me since my first day. She and Mrs. Wheatley keep saying I'm a prodigy. I'm not boasting, it's just that I've found I have a passion for words."

"It is such a strange thing for you to be tutored as if you are a daughter."

Phillis knew that now, but not at first.

When she had arrived that day and Sadie had finally settled her asthma down, she was taken to meet the rest of the family. Mrs. Wheatley pointed to a young woman, tapped her chest, and said, "Mary." And then to a young man and said, "Nathaniel."

Phillis didn't remember how long it took her to understand that they were twins—the only son and daughter of the Wheatleys—but from the moment Phillis met Mary, she knew she would like her. Mary had the kind of eyes that crinkled into a smile.

The first thing Mr. Wheatley did was to fetch a piece of

paper, an inkwell, and a quill. He said the name, "Phillis," and tapped the paper with his finger. Phillis had never used a quill, but she'd watched the *tubaab* on the ship long enough to know how he dipped, wiped, and scratched the marks. She tried it and landed a blot of ink on the paper. She wiped again and wrote a shaky P H I L L I S.

She found out later that Mary Wheatley was stunned. She could not comprehend how a sickly slave girl just off a ship from Africa could spell her name in English. Who would have taught her? Her whole life Mary had heard that Negroes could not learn—that they were not the same as whites. As she told Phillis later, if slaves could read and write, were they any less human than their masters? And, if they were fully human, what did that mean for the arguments in favor of slavery?

Her twin brother, Nathaniel, dismissed it. Mary said he figured it was some kind of trick. He was preparing to go away to finish his education, so he had little time to think about an African child who wrote English or the issue of slavery anyway.

But Mary couldn't go away to school. She would stay home. That night she asked her parents if she could tutor Phillis. Mrs. Wheatley thought it a fine idea. As she confessed later, she thought it would be a charming diversion for her daughter. Just a few days ago, before Obour arrived, she told Phillis she had no idea Mary would be such a dedicated teacher or Phillis so gifted at learning.

But here she was, a little more than a year had passed, and Phillis was telling her friend she could read. How much had changed since they said good-bye at the auction.

"I've been learning to read and write as well," Obour said.

"Oh, Obour!" Phillis breathed in deeply. "How blessed we are. You must know how few slaves are allowed to read and write."

"I heard that down South it is against the law to teach slaves to read."

Ever since Phillis understood enough English to overhear conversations, she'd heard cautionary tales about life for slaves down South.

"Um, um, um," Sadie would say, shaking her head. "You don't want to end up sold down South. Some of my people come from plantations down there, and there's a meanness you don't want to be knowing nothin' about."

Phillis knew how fortunate she and Obour were to be in Boston—if living as slaves could ever be considered fortunate. But even more, they had been blessed to find themselves in the Wheatley and Tanner families. Not many slaves were in a similar circumstance.

"Come," Obour said. "Let's go to the kitchen garden to see if the cooks need any help."

Phillis was ashamed to say that she didn't know how to help, and so she followed along.

"Can we help?" Obour asked.

Sadie looked at the two girls and laughed. "You might be able to help, Obour, but that Phillis is no bigger'n a mite. She don't know a thing about kitchen work or garden work."

Obour's cook, Dorry, laughed—a big, warm friendly laugh. "Well, she'd be old enough to work in my kitchen." She gathered up three big pumpkins in her arms and walked inside. Obour picked up the squash they had picked and followed. Phillis trailed after Sadie.

Dorry picked up a knife off the table, wiped it on her apron, and started working on the pumpkins. "When Obour came to us, she was half-starved and couldn't speak nothing but some African heathen tongue, but I managed to put her right to work." She stopped and handed Obour a bowl and a large spoon and gestured at the pumpkin halves. "She's a good help, especially now that she speaks English."

Obour started scooping the seeds and slimy strings out of the pumpkin.

"When Phillis first came, Master deposited her in the kitchen in the middle of an asthma attack. It was all I could do to steam the tightness out of that girl and get her breathing again." Sadie talked about Phillis as if she wasn't there.

"Makes you wonder," Dorry said, almost to herself, "why anyone would spend good money on a sickly child."

Phillis didn't say anything. Dorry wasn't being cruel. It was a fair question. Phillis had wondered the same thing many times.

"I asked the missus that myself one time," Sadie said. "Missus Wheatley said that when she saw Phillis clutching a ragged piece of carpet, struggling to breathe with barely anything left on her bones, she got that catch in her heart." She laughed. "You know about that catch in my mistress's heart, don't you?" She lifted the dough she was kneading, spread a handful of flour on the board, and smacked the dough back down, resuming her rhythmic motion—heel of the hands pushing forward, fingers pulling back. "She says it is God's way of getting her to do something."

Phillis had never heard the reason that Mrs. Wheatley asked Mr. Wheatley to buy her. She knew they intended to find someone to lend a hand to Mrs. Wheatley, but even Phillis knew you don't pick a sickly, scrawny seven-year-old to be a companion-helper.

"Truth be told, that catch in her heart is responsible for untold money flying out of this household," Sadie said.

Dorry chimed in, "I overheard Missus Tanner say that Susanna Wheatley is more'n generous to Reverend Occum and Reverend Whitefield as well as to her own church."

"Yes, indeed. It's that catch in her heart. Seems like all the good Lord needs do is jiggle that heart a little and He can feed a churchful of Indians or keep a preacher going far across the ocean."

Obour patted the seat next to her for Phillis.

"So I hear you can read and write almost as well as Miss Mary," Dorry said to Phillis. Without waiting for a response, she turned to Sadie. "Missus Tanner says it is a thing to behold. Your Phillis can read anything they hand her. Made my missus start teaching Obour as well."

Phillis looked at Obour and smiled.

If Obour could read, Phillis thought, then she could send Obour letters. The Wheatleys' driver, Prince, would probably see that someone delivered them. Letters were always going back and forth between the Wheatleys and the Tanners. And if Obour could learn to write . . .

"Are you daydreaming again, Phillis?" Sadie asked.

"Pardon," Phillis murmured.

"I asked what you do with yourself all day."

Phillis knew this was a trick question. The other slaves did not approve of the way Mrs. Wheatley and Mary treated Phillis. She'd overheard Lucy, the housekeeper, saying something about a lapdog. Phillis understood. They thought she was being treated like a pet instead of a person.

That wasn't the way of it—not exactly. Part of what she did could have been for their amusement. Very few people in America thought slaves could learn. In fact very few people believed slaves had souls. Most people believed Negroes were created to work for white people and would not have been able to take care of themselves.

Mrs. Wheatley and Mary did not believe that. It was one of the reasons Mary had Phillis start out by reading the Bible every day. At first Phillis worked on reading it because she longed to read. Before long, the words began to take hold in her heart and the Bible became her treasure.

As she began to read about sin, she understood. She'd seen evil firsthand. Even more, she was struck by God's plan to save sinners. Sending His own Son to be killed? She couldn't imagine that. She'd watched the pain in her own father's face as his child was taken from his arms. How God must have suffered.

She looked up and saw Dorry waiting for an answer.

"I study with Mary. I practice writing. Someday I will write letters for Mrs. Wheatley."

"Humph." Dorry gave a hard whack to another pumpkin with her butcher's knife and whacked it in half. "It somehow don't seem fitting."

As Obour finished up, Phillis jumped down off the stool. They went outside to wash the pumpkin slime off Obour.

"You asked me about Jesus," Phillis said as she held the dry rag out to her friend. "Do you follow Jesus now instead of Allah?"

"I do. Do you?"

"I never knew Allah. In our village the fathers followed Allah. It seemed to me that every time something went wrong, it was Allah's will."

"I remember. I wonder if they talk about Allah's will when they remember the capture of my mother and me."

"I follow Jesus now as well," Phillis said, answering Obour's question. "It's become the most important thing in my life."

"I'm so glad we share that faith," Obour said, squeezing her friend's hand. "It's what I've been trying to ask you all morning."

That night a small table was set for Obour and Phillis just off the dining room.

Obour kept pulling on her ear. "I can eat in the kitchen with the servants," she said to Mrs. Tanner.

"No, Obour. You sit here and keep Phillis company this time. Mrs. Wheatley plans to have Phillis read."

When everyone settled in the dining room and the soup had been served, Lucy came and served soup to Obour and Phillis.

"How can you stand to eat here and feel the other slaves' resentment?" Obour leaned across the table so she could whisper, "I mean Lucy doesn't say anything, but you can tell by the way she set the bowl down that she disapproves."

"It's worse than that. I don't usually sit here."

"Oh, I misunderstood. I didn't know you took meals in

the kitchen with everyone else." Obour sat with her hand hovering over the silverware as if not sure what spoon to use.

"Take from the outside," Phillis said. "That's the soup spoon." She took a taste of her soup. "You didn't misunderstand. I don't get to eat in the kitchen. I sit at the dining table with the family."

Obour put her spoon down. "Oh, Phillis." The tone of her words spoke deep sympathy.

"Mrs. Wheatley and Mary have been so good to me—treating me almost like a daughter of the family—I would hate for them to know how difficult it makes it for me." She laid her spoon on the plate. "You can understand what an odd position it puts me in with the other servants as well as with guests of the Wheatleys."

"So whenever guests come, you sit at this table?"

Phillis nodded her head. "I always think of a saying Mr. Wheatley uses, 'Neither fish nor fowl.'"

They continued to eat and visit, ignoring Lucy's comments and spills during service. When dessert came, Phillis folded her napkin and laid it beside her plate.

"You are not going to eat the pumpkin pie?" Obour asked.

"I will be called to read during dessert." She stood to walk into the dining room. "Don't let Lucy clear away my dessert until I get back."

Obour laughed and made as if to guard it.

The next morning Obour helped pack the hired carriages that would take the Tanners to the dock. As her mistress and master took leave of the Wheatleys, Obour found Phillis.

"I must take leave now, but we shall be back."

"I'm so glad you came. You are my one true friend."

"I'm glad I came as well. I understand so much better now."

"You do?" Phillis didn't know what Obour understood.

"I'd heard through servants' gossip that you were pampered. I heard them say you were like a pet and you didn't even know you weren't part of the family."

"They said all that?" Phillis felt ashamed.

"Maybe I shouldn't have repeated what I'd heard, but now I see the true way of it."

One of the drivers called to Obour that they were ready to leave.

"I must go, but I think you are brave, Phillis. The kitchen is the most comfortable place for a slave. You've been denied that comfort because you are studying—you are proving that Negroes can learn. I can see that Mrs. Wheatley is allowing you to learn to read and write and to meet her guests so she can prove that we slaves are humans—we are capable of learning and we have souls."

Phillis hugged her. "Yes, we have souls, and Jesus loves us. I'm so glad you came."

Obour hugged her hard. "You are doing an important thing, Phillis. I will pray for you."

Deep Calleth unto Deep

Boston, 1765

"Phillis." Lucy rapped loudly on the attic door. "Get up. Mary wants to start your lessons early."

"Come in, Lucy."

She opened the door and pushed Phillis's breakfast tray onto the small table. It smelled so good—cornmeal mush with molasses, cider, and a small pot of tea.

Phillis had been sitting at her small desk. She closed her Bible.

"Oh, you're awake." Lucy sounded disappointed.

"Yes, but I'll eat and dress quickly." Phillis wished Lucy would stay for a few minutes. "Did you already eat?"

Lucy wrinkled her nose. "Before we serve the house? No."

Lucy wasn't the only one of the servants who often addressed Phillis as if she were a slow-witted child. But maybe she was slow-witted enough to want to mend fences with Lucy.

"I wondered if you wanted to join me. There's enough here, and you can tell me about your good news." Phillis had heard Lucy had asked permission to marry the groundskeeper.

"And what are you supposing Sadie would say if she ended up with two of us taking meals upstairs?" She curled her lip as she mimicked the way Mrs. Wheatley said "taking meals upstairs."

Phillis gave up. "You're right. It was foolish of me to ask. Thank you for bringing my breakfast."

Lucy left, and Phillis picked at the food on the tray. She didn't blame Lucy. How would she feel if she had been a hardworking slave and the family bought a new slave and installed her in a room upstairs, let her eat and study with the family, and made the rest of them wait on her like she was a lady of the house?

How she wished Obour lived closer.

But there was no time for wishing. If Mary wanted to start lessons early, Phillis needed to get dressed. She took her everyday clothes out of the clothes press and set them on her bed. How different colonial dress was from her mother's *mbubba*. African dress was colorful and comfortable. And it was never too hot because it consisted of wrapped lengths of cotton. When the sun got hotter you just unwrapped some.

What made her think of Africa? She'd been here in Boston for nearly five years.

She slipped the petticoat over her head and fastened the tapes to close it, arranging it over her nightdress.

If she were still in her village, she'd probably have her

own groundnut field now. How odd to remember the word, groundnut. Here in America she called them peanuts. She hadn't thought about groundnuts for years.

She folded the flounce of her nightdress sleeve tightly against her arm so she could slip her jacket over it. She did the other arm and then arranged the flounces to peek out of the sleeve. She tightly laced the ties across her chest and hooked the stomacher over the opening. Maybe she was thinking about Africa because everything was so complicated here in America. Even getting dressed. Sadie and Lucy wore simpler clothing—a homespun dress, an apron, a handkerchief for tucking into the neckline, and a cap. Not all the slaves wore simple clothing. Her dresses were not nearly as ornate and complicated as the clothes worn by Prince, the Wheatleys' driver, who wore full livery.

Still it made much more sense to wear a *mbubba* that could be washed in the stream than to wear clothes of silk or wool that could never be washed. How much time did Lucy spend brushing, spotting, and sunning clothes to keep them fresh?

She smiled at the memory of her first night in the house. Sadie gave her a linen nightgown to wear to bed. The next day she found out she was expected to put her day clothes on top of it. She found out later that it was because the linens would be washed, boiled, starched, and ironed regularly. The fancy clothing never actually touched her body, helping to preserve it.

Phillis finished her morning toilette at the dressing table, picking and arranging her tight curls and putting on her morning cap. She tidied her room and went downstairs to the library.

"Morning, Phillis." Mary stood at one of the bookcases. "I thought we'd get started early today. Mother will join us in the morning room for tea after she's finished her correspondence, so I want to discuss what you'll be doing this week."

Phillis headed over to her own stack of books.

"No Milton today," Mary said. "If I didn't nudge you toward other titles you'd spend every day with Milton and Alexander Pope, wouldn't you?"

Phillis laughed. "'Twouldn't be a bad way to spend the day."

"Look what I found for you." Mary held out a volume to Phillis. "It's Homer, translated by Alexander Pope."

Phillis reached for the book reverently. "Oh, Mary." What was it about a book that made her long for what she'd discover inside the pages?

"We need to begin your Latin before long, but for now, I know you will enjoy Homer."

Phillis couldn't have wished for a more dedicated tutor than Mary. Ever since she arrived at the Wheatley home Mary had tutored her. Even now when Mary was newly betrothed to the Reverend John Lathrop, she still set lessons for Phillis, listened to her read, and corrected her writing. Mary organized lessons in geography, history, the Bible, English, and classical literature. It was an education few white girls were offered, let alone a slave girl.

"Homer." Phillis took the book into both hands. "I will begin to read it right away."

She curled up in a chair, opened the book, and began reading the *Odyssey*. Time slipped away. Here was a storyteller— a *griot* who used written words.

Lucy knocked and entered the room, giving a quick curtsey to Mary. Phillis looked up. She didn't know how much time had passed. She'd been reading, and Mary had been writing letters.

"Mrs. Wheatley is ready for tea in the morning room," Lucy said, opening the door wide.

Phillis took her book and trailed Mary out of the library. Lucy followed and closed the door behind her.

"We have a busy day ahead of us today," Mrs. Wheatley said as they joined her. "But first, tell me how your studies went."

Mary greeted her mother with a kiss on the cheek. "There is less and less for me to do these days. I'm afraid the student will soon surpass the teacher."

"Come, Phillis. Sit here beside me." Mrs. Wheatley gathered her skirts so Phillis could sit. "Your progress is nothing short of remarkable. I do worry about your health, though." She put a hand on Phillis's cheek. "Despite everything, you are still thin and you continue to have the asthma. I want you to spend time in the garden as well as in your books."

"Yes, ma'am." Phillis knew Mrs. Wheatley worried about her, but no matter how much she tried to fatten herself up it didn't work. She'd probably always be thin, but she loved Mrs. Wheatley's concern.

"I see you've been writing letters, Mother." Mary went over and picked up a stack. "I've written a few as well. Shall I give them all to Prince?"

"Yes, after we've had tea."

Lucy brought the tea tray, and Mary poured out. She

handed cups to her mother and Phillis. Sadie had made tiny custard tarts to go with the tea.

"Tonight Reverend Occum will be coming to dinner. He and Reverend Whitaker will leave presently for England and Scotland to raise money for the Indian school. Phillis, would you read the Bible for us again?"

"Yes, ma'am."

Mrs. Wheatley put her hand over Phillis's hand. "It may appear that we are showing you off to all visitors, but it is more than vain boasting. I have a reason for doing this, and I want you to understand."

Mrs. Wheatley's kindness to her had never changed in all the years she'd lived there. But explaining her actions to a slave? That had never happened before.

"There are far too many who believe Negroes have no need of salvation. I know you've heard it—that slaves have no souls. It's nonsense, but we are so consumed with the question of slavery that when we discover that our slaves are just like us, it can be discomforting. I want people to see with fresh eyes. With each new guest at our table, we are changing minds."

"So, Mother, are you saying you no longer believe in slavery?"

"No." She sounded surprised by the question as if she'd never thought about it. "I don't know." She shook her curls as if to clear her head. "Besides it little matters what a woman believes, because slavery is a business institution. The men deal with business, and we have precious little voice."

Phillis didn't say anything.

"What I'm most concerned with is the Lord's business.

Slave or free, Indian or Negro, it doesn't matter to me. All of us need salvation. That's what I'm trying to change."

"But Mother, surely you don't need to change Samson Occum's mind."

"No. Reverend Occum's here because he wants to meet Phillis before he goes abroad." She turned to explain to Phillis. "Reverend Occum is a Mohegan Indian himself. He came to salvation during the Great Awakening. He felt called to preach, so he secured an education and became a missionary to his own people. He is a powerful orator."

"He's now seeking additional funds for his Indian school." Mary smiled at her mother and waved an envelope. "And you can guess who is supplying a portion of those funds."

Mrs. Wheatley blushed. "Mary, don't be tactless."

Phillis couldn't wait to meet Reverend Occum. So far, all the ministers she'd met were white. How fitting that God would call an Indian for the Indians.

* * *

"This is a delicious dinner, Mrs. Wheatley." Reverend Occum folded his napkin. "Thank you for the support you've given to our school. As you can imagine, it's never been an easy task securing funds."

"So now you embark on a trip abroad to raise funds?" Mr. Wheatley asked. "Do you have your return trip booked?"

"Not at this time. I need to be free to go where the Lord leads. I'll secure passage closer to the time of return."

"If my ship, *The London Packet*, is in port, please feel free to travel at my expense."

"Thank you, Mr. Wheatley. You and Mrs. Wheatley are most generous."

"So you'll be preaching in the Scottish and English pulpits?"

"Yes. I'll be preaching some three hundred times from what I understand. I'm scheduled to speak to King George and meet with our benefactor, William Legge, Earl of Dartmouth."

Phillis, who usually didn't speak at the table, gasped. "You will give three hundred sermons?"

Reverend Occum smiled. "As long as my voice holds out. You will remember me in prayer, Phillis, won't you?"

"I will," she promised. She had loved hearing the stories Samson Occum told at the table. When she left Africa, she thought she'd never see a *griot* again, but she'd learned that storytellers flourish in all cultures, from ancient Greece to the Gambia to the colonies.

"And now," he said, "I understand you are going to read for us."

Phillis pushed back her chair, stood up, and moved a few steps away from the table to a small occasional table where she'd laid her Bible. She opened it to Psalm 42 and read in a clear voice: "As the hart panteth after the water brooks, so panteth my soul after thee, O God. My soul thirsteth for God, for the living God: when shall I come and appear before God?"

She paused and breathed in deeply. The words touched her soul in some deep mysterious way every time she read the passage. She pictured the hart—her gazelle—panting after water during the dry season. That was exactly how she longed for God.

She took a breath and continued, "My tears have been my meat day and night, while they continually say unto me, Where is thy God?"

She paused and looked at Reverend Occum. His eyes were closed, and he, too, inhaled deeply through his nose, pulling the very words inside. She continued reading the psalm, and when she got to the verse, "Deep calleth unto deep at the noise of thy waterspouts: all thy waves and thy billows are gone over me," she breathed a silent prayer for the minister's safety on the ocean voyage. She knew how fierce the ocean could be.

She finished the psalm and sat down. The last words, "for I shall yet praise him, who is the health of my countenance, and my God," seemed to resonate in the room.

Mrs. Wheatley closed her eyes and tipped her head ever so slightly at her. Phillis's heart swelled—high praise, indeed.

"Daughter, those words are a balm to my soul," Reverend Occum said. "I heard more than a young slave reading words by rote. I heard words that had seared your very soul."

Phillis laid her Bible down, took her chair, and sat very still. She had to concentrate to catch her breath.

After dinner in her room, Phillis penned her very first letter by flickering candlelight, a letter to Reverend Occum. She needed to finish it that very night while her thoughts were fresh. She would send it on the next ship so it could follow

Reverend Occum to England. She used her best penmanship and ended the letter with, "Wishing you all possible success, I remain your humble servant, Phillis Wheatley."

She couldn't stop thinking about the stories he told—of the Indian students at his school as well as the ones who could not enroll but who also longed for an education. If only she had money, she'd have put some into the envelope like Mrs. Wheatley, but her promise of prayer and her best wishes would have to suffice.

8

The Memory of You Forever

Boston, 1766

*I*f King George doesn't repeal this wretched Stamp Act, I don't know what will happen." Mr. Wheatley pulled his napkin off his lap, pushed his chair back, and began pacing.

"John, please," Mrs. Wheatley whispered, "we have guests. It's not good for digestion."

Nathaniel winked at Mary and Phillis. He was home from college. All three of them knew that once Mr. Wheatley was riled up, there was no stopping him. His business associates, Messrs. Hussey and Coffin, were just as exasperated.

"I can't keep quiet. This new tax is injurious to business. Who ever thought of having to buy a stamp in order to have the right to print a newspaper, create a legal document, distribute a broadside, or even write a letter."

"It goes against the grain," said Mr. Coffin. "We were promised that no taxes would be levied on the colonies without a vote. Aren't we Englishmen still? Don't we have a right to consent?"

"Would anyone care for another slice of roast turkey?" Mrs. Wheatley tugged on her husband's arm to get him to sit down.

"The trouble is, England decides to wage a Seven Years' War to add to its holdings and we Americans are expected to fork over the money to replenish their coffers."

Phillis could see that the conversation was only building. She looked over at a flustered Mrs. Wheatley and smiled a look of sympathy.

"John, this is bound to end in nothing more than indigestion."

Nathaniel spoke up. "There's plenty to discuss with the Stamp Act—we've been debating it at school. Some feel it will lead to a rupture with England if it's not repealed."

Taxing letters. Phillis shook her head. Of all things to tax, why did King George want to tax writing? She remembered the first time she discovered written words—the name of the ship stamped on a crate on a slave ship—a word that would end up being her name.

Yes, writing was powerful. Someone should have warned the king that you may be able to tax sugar or molasses, but when you try to tax the written word, you've grabbed a leopard by the tail.

"So, Mr. Hussey, tell us about your shipwreck." Mrs. Wheatley tried valiantly to steer the conversation away from heartburn-producing topics.

"Well, I'm not a weak-kneed soul, but that was as close as I ever want to come to Neptune's lair."

Phillis put her fork down and leaned forward. She could always tell when a good story was coming.

"We'd pushed off from Nantucket in fair weather. We weren't that far into our trip when a squall came up, the like of which I never saw."

"'Twas late for a storm that violent, was it not?" Mr. Wheatley had apparently moved past the Stamp Act.

"Yes. At first the boat tossed but seemed to be holding. The sound of the wind was deafening."

Mr. Coffin interrupted. "We knew well the number of shipwrecks along the Cape Cod coast between Chatham and Provincetown. 'Tis no mystery why they call that stretch the Ocean Graveyard."

"As we were slammed repeatedly into sandbars, we kept waiting to hear the call 'Ship ashore. All hands perishing!'" Mr. Hussey leaned forward. "How many times have we heard that alarm ourselves?"

"How did you survive?" Phillis hadn't meant to interrupt the story, but she had to know. Here these men were seated across the table eating roast turkey with them. Everyone knew that a ship hitting the sandbar was fair pickings for the wreckers.

"Only by the grace of God," Mr. Hussey said. "Only by the grace of God."

"Aye," said Mr. Coffin. "A huge wave came in and scraped us off the sandbar and back out to sea, righting us in the process. At the same time, the squall seemed to ease and we limped on toward Boston."

"Incredible," Nathaniel said. "How many sailors end up on the Ocean Graveyard and live to tell about it?"

"'Twas Providence, pure and simple." Mr. Hussey lifted his hands to heaven. "We figured we'd made our beds in the depths."

Phillis couldn't stop thinking about their words. When it came time for her to read, she chose Psalm 69. She opened her Bible and began to read, "Deliver me out of the mire, and let me not sink: let me be delivered from them that hate me, and out of the deep waters. Let not the waterflood overflow me, neither let the deep swallow me up, and let not the pit shut her mouth upon me."

That night in her room, Phillis once again took pen to paper and let the words flow out of her heart and through her quill. Maybe it was the Psalms or the poetry of Alexander Pope that inspired her, but instead of a letter, this time she began to compose poetry. She worked until light began to streak the sky.

She tucked the page away and blew out the candle, but she continued to work on it the next day. When she finally felt it was ready, she brought it to Mary, who was sitting at her desk writing a letter.

Mary took the page from Phillis and read it. She looked up at Phillis.

"Did you write this?" Mary said.

"Yes. Can't you tell by my penmanship?"

"No, I mean did you write this yourself, not copy it from somewhere?" Mary looked down at the poem, reading it once more, mouthing the words.

"Come with me." She took the poem with her. Phillis trailed behind.

"Mother. Listen to this." She hadn't even knocked at the door of the morning room. She just opened the door and burst in with Phillis trailing behind.

Phillis could feel her chest tighten. *Relax.*

"Phillis wrote this poem to Messrs. Hussey and Coffin to commemorate their narrow escape. I won't read you the whole poem, but listen to these lines:

Did haughty Eolus with Contempt look down
With aspect windy, and a study'd Frown?
Regard them not:—the Great Supreme, the Wise,
Intends for something hidden from our eyes . . .

Mrs. Wheatley put her hands on her desk and stood up. "Let me see the whole poem."

She stood there reading, while Phillis's heart thudded. She read it through once, then looked at Phillis without saying anything. Then she read it again.

"I don't know what to say." She kept shaking her head. "This is momentous, child. Do you have any idea what this means?"

Phillis shook her head.

"It is one thing to learn how to read and write—not trifling, mind you, but many have done likewise. This, however, has never been done to my knowledge."

"What, Mother?"

"Think on it, Mary. This child came from darkest Africa only five years ago. She had not a word of English. That she learned the language and became proficient reading and writing it is miracle enough, but consider . . ." She began pacing.

Phillis had never seen Mrs. Wheatley pace. She was every inch the lady and, as she would have reminded Phillis, ladies don't pace.

"Poetry—good poetry—is one of the highest linguistic art forms. Can it be taught? I think not."

"Well, I certainly can't teach it since I'm not a practitioner of the art." Mary put an arm around her mother and led her to her chair.

"Phillis, how did you do this?" Mrs. Wheatley put down the poem and reached out to take both of Phillis's hands in hers.

Phillis didn't know to explain. How did one stand in a parlor in Boston and explain African talking drums, *griots*, a song for a dead gazelle, and the longing to create her own praise songs? "I took my pen and tried to capture the narrative in images like Alexander Pope would have done. I used his closed couplets."

She knew it was more than that, but she had no way to explain. How could she explain that she drew from experiences during her time on the pitching, rolling deck of a slave ship? Mary and Mrs. Wheatley seemed to think her life began on that pier in Boston.

"This poem will be published."

"Mother, how can you promise that? Especially with the Stamp Act in effect—the print world is in an uproar."

"I will see to it. It may take some money, and I may have to make calls on influential persons, but it will be published."

She stood up and rang the bell for Lucy. When the girl

came in, Mrs. Wheatley began giving instructions like a general. "Tell Prince I want him to go to the stationers. I need him to buy paper, vellum, ink, and some fine-nib quills. When you are done with that, bring extra candles and firewood up to Phillis's room. I need it warm in case the muses visit her in the night."

Lucy narrowed her eyes at Phillis as she left the room.

Phillis continued to write poetry. Now when guests came to dinner, she recited poetry. Most believed that a Negro had never before written poetry. Phillis didn't know about that, but she did know that in Africa much of the history was related through song and meter.

At one dinner party, shortly after the ridiculous Butter Rebellion at Harvard—where the men walked out of school, protesting the quality of the butter they were served—Phillis shared a poem she wrote to the men who studied there.

To you Bright youths! He points the heights of heav'n
To you, the knowledge of the depths profound

As she read all the verses, those at the table broke into smiles. As Mary pointed out, what a delightful irony for a thirteen-year-old slave to be admonishing Harvard men to embrace the opportunity for an education.

"It seems to make no sense for those students to be consumed with their own comfort when the colonies are laboring under the Stamp Act." Mr. Wheatley's businesses had suffered under the unfair taxation.

Phillis shuddered. She remembered the riots that broke out to protest the Stamp Act. They destroyed the Stamp Building and smashed out the windows of the stamp master's house. The yelling, the torches, the anger—it was all frightening.

"Did you not hear the news?" One of Mr. Wheatley's business associates put his hands on the table to raise himself to a standing position. "Let me announce it here, then: The Stamp Act was repealed as of March 18th."

"Hear, hear!" several men jumped up and shouted. For once Mrs. Wheatley did not admonish them.

That night, in her room, Phillis wrote a poem to King George, lauding him for repealing the Stamp Act. She poured out her hopes for an end to the troubles between England and her colonies and thanked him for his favors:

Midst the remembrance of thy favours past,
The meanest peasants most admire the last.

The last favor, of course, was the repeal of the Stamp Act.

❧   ❧   ❧   ❧

The Wheatley mansion had been festooned with holly and ivy in preparation for Christmas. Nathaniel would be home and Mary's fiancé, John Lathrop, would be visiting. Sadie had been cooking for days, and the house smelled rich with spices.

Phillis had just finished dressing for the day when someone knocked on her door. Since Lucy had already delivered her breakfast tray, she opened the door, rather than call out her customary, "Come in."

Mary stood at the door with lips pressed together.

"Is everything all right, Mary?"

"Yes, but Mother needs you downstairs immediately."

"Immediately? Are you sure everything is all right?"

Mary didn't answer. She just pressed her lips together more tightly.

Phillis followed her downstairs, trying to guess what could be the matter. She ran through everything she could think of: illness, political trouble, financial trouble. None of those could be described as "all right."

Mary led her into the parlor where the whole family had assembled.

"I have something you need to see." Mrs. Wheatley had her hands behind her back like a schoolgirl.

Phillis couldn't imagine what it was. An early Christmas gift?

"Look. You are a published poet." She held out a copy of the *Newport Mercury*, dated December 21, 1767. Printed right on the page of the newspaper was her poem about the near-shipwreck of Messrs. Hussey and Coffin.

Phillis took the paper in her shaking hands and let Mary help her sit down. "How did—When did you—" She fell silent. "Thank you, Mrs. Wheatley. I know this is entirely your doing."

"It is not entirely my doing. I helped get it to the right people, but had not the quality been there, nothing could have been done to get it published."

"I'm having trouble taking this in," Phillis confessed. She remembered the day she asked her mother if a woman could ever become a *griot*.

It was as if Mrs. Wheatley had heard her thoughts. "Phillis, you will be remembered forever as the first Negro poetess in America and one of the first women to be published in these colonies."

Phillis remembered the last line of the praise song she made for the gazelle all those years ago: "I hold the memory of you forever."

9

'Twas Mercy

Boston, 1768

*P*hillis, would you kindly read your newest poem for our
guests?" Mrs. Wheatley motioned to Lucy to pull out
Phillis's chair.

As Phillis stood to read, she could hear the faint cluck of
the tongue from Lucy that told of her disgust. Phillis had
been part of the Wheatley household for almost seven years
now, and though Sadie had warmed up to her and accepted
her strange position in the family, Lucy never had.

Phillis had tried many times to befriend Lucy, but the
housekeeper had turned a cold shoulder. Phillis had overheard too many comments over the years to hold any hope of
a truce. Things like: "She don't know if she be white or
black." Or "She's gettin' too big for her britches. 'Cept when
she came, if I recollect, she didn't have so much as a pair of
britches to cover her skinny self."

Sadie would always shush her, but the words burned like acid and kept burning long afterward.

Phillis spent many hours praying about the problem. How was she to do the work she loved, connect with the people Mrs. Wheatley wanted her to connect with, and still be one of the servants?

She knew she was a slave, just like Prince, Sadie, Lucy, and the others. Sometimes it smoldered in her. When she read the Bible and felt the hunger of Moses for his people and for freedom, she burned with the same hunger. She read about the state of slaves in the colonies. She knew she had it easy and the other servants in the Wheatley house had it far better than most, but one thing was missing—freedom.

Her job now, though, was to help show the world that Negroes could be educated, could do any job a white person could do, including being published. She battled this every day. After all, she was not only a slave but she was a girl. Women didn't have the opportunity to have the same education as men, and the words women wrote certainly weren't considered for publication. Every time she thought about it, she realized it wasn't so different than it had been in her village. She remembered her mother's silence when she asked if a girl could ever become a *griot*.

Sometimes she thought if she could just explain to Lucy what was at stake, perhaps she would understand.

Probably not.

But she never forgot that her most important task was to help the colonists see that Negroes had a need for salvation—for Jesus. So many honestly believed that people from Africa did not have souls. How many times had she heard men say,

"They were made for work. We need to take care of them. Without their masters they'd starve."

How she wished she could see those men fending for themselves in Africa. Her people would probably say the same thing about them.

But since she'd found faith—a true and living, breathing faith—she needed to bring along her brothers and sisters. Colonists must understand that in God's eyes they were all alike.

"Child, are you going to read, or are you going to stand there woolgathering?"

She didn't know how long she'd been standing. *Dear Lord*, she prayed silently, *help my poem open eyes.*

'Twas mercy brought me from my *Pagan* land,
Taught my benighted soul to understand
That there's a God, that there's a *Saviour* too:
Once I redemption neither sought nor knew.
Some view our sable race with scornful eye,
"Their colour is a diabolic die."
Remember, *Christians*, *Negros*, black as *Cain*,
May be refin'd, and join th' angelic train.

Mrs. Wheatley wiped her eyes as Phillis finished reading. Everyone around the table clapped, some vigorously, some politely. Phillis knew these words were hard for some to swallow, but it was truth. God sent His Son to the slaves as well as to all the well-dressed businessmen at this table.

"Phillis, please leave your poem here on the table so that we may study and discuss it." Mrs. Wheatley smiled at her.

"And will you go into the kitchen and tell Sadie to hold dessert for a little while?"

Phillis took her leave quietly, knowing Mrs. Wheatley would press them to consider the things Phillis wrote. *In a way, I'm a missionary to the influential people of Boston on behalf of my people.* She caught herself and laughed at the thought. Maybe at fifteen she was not quite a missionary, but she knew that her whole life she'd longed to tell stories and create the poems she used to call songs. Now she was doing it.

As she approached the kitchen she could hear Lucy talking. "She called us a 'sable race' and said our color is a 'diabolic dye.' That means from the devil, doesn't it?"

"Um humh," Sadie said. "It does, but surely she didn't mean it like that."

"I tell you, she did. She said ''twas mercy' that took her from her 'pagan land.'" Lucy's voice became even more strident. "'Pagan land,' she said."

"Are you sure?" Sadie sounded doubtful.

"As sure as I'm standing here. She's gone and sold us down the river again. She's no different from the Africans what sold their own brothers."

Phillis felt her chest tighten. Lucy had it all wrong. The poem was about mercy and salvation. Phillis would never forget the horrors she endured—being ripped from the heart of her parents, the beatings and, worse, the stench of the slave ship—but what if she had never come and met Jesus?

How could they not understand? She felt the breath being squeezed from her lungs as she sank to the floor with a thud.

She opened her eyes to see Sadie kneeling beside her. "Relax, child. Relax." The cook propped her up to a sitting position. "Lucy, don't stand there gaping. Run and get the Missus."

Phillis had been in bed for almost a fortnight. She had never had a bout of the asthma last so long or develop into such congestion. Either Sadie or Mary brought her meals to her room. Much of the time she'd slept, but she was finally beginning to gain some strength.

She longed to have someone to talk to. How she wished Obour lived near. She had been thinking of her friend for days. As she slept, she often dreamed they sat under a baobab tree. Once she had a far-too-real dream of the time they spent together on the deck of the slave ship, sitting between the crates.

Maybe, since she couldn't be with Obour, she could write to her instead. She eased herself to a sitting position. She felt like a newborn gazelle—weak and wobbly. She inched her way to the side of the bed. The dizziness and shortness of breath did not come, so she walked the three steps to her desk and sat at her chair. It felt so good.

A sheet of paper lay on the desktop. It must have been there, waiting for words, since before she fell ill. She took her pen, dipped it in the inkwell, and began to write, shaky at first.

Dear Obour,

I have been ill these past weeks but have longed to talk to you. I have no one to whom I can unburden my heart.

Just before I fell ill, I overheard talk in the kitchen. Lucy condemned me with great fervor. It did not catch me by surprise, but it wounded more than I would have thought.

I am not ignorant of the state of things.

To the whites I am a curiosity—an amusement. I am not white enough to have my work held up against the standard for all poetry. To the slaves I am not Negro enough—I am kept from their culture and community. Forget that I came on the same cruel slave ship. And to the Africans I am not African enough, even though I may have been born in their very village.

Do I sound peevish?

Well, praise God, I do not have to be Christian enough to be loved and accepted by my heavenly Father. I humbly write the words that flow from my heart, through my quill and onto my paper—words that almost seem to be breathed by the Holy Spirit.

So my words are accepted by the only critic I long to please.

Say we will see each other soon.

Your friend and your sister,
Phillis

She folded the letter. Where had her strength gone? She felt so drained she could barely stumble back to bed.

Sadie came in with a tray. "How are you, child?" she asked, coming to lay a hand on Phillis's cheek.

"Sadie, why are you coming all the way up here to bring my food?" Sadie wasn't young. To reach Phillis's bedroom she had to walk up the grand staircase and then up the attic steps carrying a tray of food.

Sadie set down the tray and rubbed her back. "Um, um, um. Are you saying I'm not a spring chicken?"

Phillis smiled but didn't answer.

"I'm so glad you're awake today and more like yourself. I been wanting to talk." Sadie sat on the chair by the bed. "I reckoned you heard what Lucy said the night you fell ill. It made you so troubled that your breath caught in your chest, didn't it?" She pulled the cover up and helped Phillis sit up. "I've been coming to tend you 'cause I don't need to have Lucy upsetting you no more."

Phillis didn't have enough strength to say much. "I heard her words, but she didn't understand. And I found I didn't have breath to explain myself."

"I know, child. Mrs. Wheatley been talking 'bout what an impression you made on her guests." Sadie spread a napkin across Phillis's stomach. "One of those guests was a preacher-friend of the Missus, and I hear he been preachin' up a storm. Miss Mary says that storm sounds mighty similar to the words you brewed in your poem."

Phillis smiled but didn't say anything. If her poem had wounded her own people—if they didn't understand what she meant—then she wished she could take it all back.

"That Lucy, she just says what she thinks without thinking 'bout anybody else." Sadie dipped a spoon into the porridge, and Phillis stopped her.

"I can feed myself now."

"That's good. It's 'bout time you start perkin' up." She stepped back and put a hand on her hip. "Now I don't want you paying Lucy no mind. She just speaks out, that one."

Phillis put down her spoon. "Will she ever like me, Sadie? I never meant to live high and mighty, like she says. I'm only trying to set my hand to the work God's set before me."

"I don't have an answer for that, child. I do know that if someone bears a grudge against you, the best thing a body can do is start in to praying for them."

"I should be praying for her?" Phillis thought for a minute. Why didn't she think of that? She knew how powerful prayer could be. During the time she'd known Lucy there had been so many things she could have prayed for her. Like when she married and then, just a few months ago, when she had her little baby boy.

She should have been praying for her instead of harboring a hurt feeling that Lucy hadn't shared any of those events with her. She hadn't even seen the baby yet. "Sadie, thank you," Phillis said, as she reached for the spoon. "'Tis what I'll do. I'll pray for Lucy."

After she'd finished eating and Sadie had cleared away the tray, she got up again and went to her desk. She read the letter she'd written Obour one more time and then folded it in half and ripped it into tiny pieces.

Instead of complaining, I'm going to start praying.

Freedom's Cause

Boston, 1770

"There's a mob out there, I tell you. An angry mob." Nathaniel had run into the house without even brushing the snow off his greatcoat. "Where's Father?"

"He's in the library," Phillis said as she went to the door to look out.

"Oh no you don't." Nathaniel put his hand on the closed door. "This crowd is worked up, and even if they weren't, it's bitter cold with snow deep on the ground. With your lungs, you'd be in bed for a fortnight."

"But I heard the yelling from my room and came down to investigate. What is it about?"

"I can guess what it's about without any explanation." Mr. Wheatley had overheard Nathaniel and come into the vestibule.

"It's some kind of altercation between the redcoats and

the citizens." Nathaniel took off his coat and hat, hanging them on the hall tree.

"Nathaniel!" His mother joined them. She cupped his face in her hands and kissed him on the cheek. "How very nice to see you."

The noise out on the street got even louder.

"What's that commotion?" Mrs. Wheatley asked.

"It's some kind of riot out there, and I'll tell you one thing. This unrest is not good for business." Mr. Wheatley began to pace. "Where is this going to end?"

Phillis had wondered the same thing. She wasn't as worried about business as she was about this country of hers. King George didn't understand the colonists—of that she was sure. Instead of allowing these Americans some leeway, he kept tightening down his rule. He was strangling the colonies. Did it surprise anyone that the independent colonists would push back?

"With so many taxes levied by the king, is it any wonder that people are rebelling?" Mr. Wheatley continued to pace. Nothing got him quite so worked up these days.

"Please sit down, John." Mrs. Wheatley took him by the hand and led him into the sitting room. "If you don't calm down you're going to have an apoplectic fit."

"We'll weather this, Father," Nathaniel said. "It's just getting harder and harder to stay neutral. How does one continue to be loyal to England when one feels the blood of a free American running through his veins?"

"It's that blood surging through American hearts that's causing all this chaos." Mr. Wheatley put his head in his hands. "If everyone could stop being so hotheaded."

Phillis understood the hotheadedness. Just a few weeks ago, a group of American patriots went to the home of a loyalist —a man they suspected of being a traitor to the colonies. A shouting match broke out, and the accused traitor, fearing for his home and family, took a gun and shot into the crowd. He struck a child—an eleven-year-old named Christopher Seider.

Phillis couldn't abide the violence. She took up her pen and wrote:

> In heaven's eternal court it was decreed
> How the first martyr for the cause should bleed
> To clear the country of the hated brood
> He whet his courage for the common good

She continued writing until she'd composed a full elegy for this boy she considered the first martyr of the revolution. Since then she had allowed her own blood to cool. She had remembered Sadie's suggestion to pray for Lucy and decided to apply it to all her enemies. She had begun to pray for the king and for his ministers and soldiers. She prayed that they would understand the colonists' hunger for freedom.

"Whatever is happening?" Mary came rushing through the door, followed by her fiancé, Reverend John Lathrop. "I thought we'd never get home. We had to have Prince leave the carriage down the street and we walked. King Street is filled with soldiers and townspeople."

Nathaniel told his sister and John what little he knew as the shouting got louder.

"Let me get Sadie to brew some tea," Mrs. Wheatley said. "Come everyone, sit and—"

The unmistakable sound of shots rang out—volley after volley.

"Oh, no! Lord, please, no." Mr. Wheatley put his head in his hands once more.

That night no one seemed inclined to retire in the Wheatley household. Nathaniel and John Lathrop went out to see what happened. When they came back, the sag of their bodies told the tale.

"Three men are dead," Nathaniel said, "including Crispus Attucks. Two more are gravely wounded."

Phillis gasped. She had met Crispus. He was half Negro, half Indian—a sailor and a free man of color.

"It should never have started," John said. "One of the hothead apprentices began taunting a British soldier about, of all things, his master's unpaid wig bill."

"You know how tense everyone is at this point, redcoats and patriots alike. What a stupid thing to do." Mr. Wheatley wanted the trouble, as he called it, to go away. As he said so many times, it was bad for business.

"After the taunts went on for some time, the soldier struck the apprentice on the side of his head with the butt of a gun. The apprentice's friend jumped into the fray, and the ruckus attracted a crowd." John sat down and clasped his hands.

"I can imagine the rest." Mr. Wheatley started pacing.

"I just don't see where this is going," Mrs. Wheatley said.

Phillis did. The more she'd been out and about, the more she heard the cries for freedom from taxation, freedom from tyranny, freedom from England. The king was too far removed to understand these colonists.

But Phillis had no trouble understanding. Freedom. Was there some innate hunger in each man for freedom? There had been slaves since at least the time of Joseph in Egypt, and yet everyone yearned to be free. Look at what Moses and the children of Israel risked for freedom. And many of them remembered the kind of enslavement she had—plenty of food, comfortable lodgings, captors who became like family. Yet the heart still beat for freedom.

Phillis excused herself and went up to her room. There would be no sleep for her on this night. She took out her pen and a fresh sheet of paper and began to write. When she finished, she had put her impressions on paper in the form of a poem she called "On the Affray in King-Street, on the Evening of the 5th of March."

In part, she wrote:

> Long as in Freedom's Cause the wise contend,
> Dear to your unity shall Fame extend;
> While to the World, the letter's Stone shall tell,
> How Caldwell, Attucks, Gray and Mav'rick fell.

When she finally finished her poem, she didn't even bother to take off her day clothes. She just draped herself across her bed, shoes dangling off one end, arms the other, and fell asleep.

She must have slept long past morning, because the next thing she remembered was being shaken by Lucy.

"Wake up. Are you sick?"

She shook the sleep from her groggy head. "No. I wrote for many hours and then just collapsed in sleep."

"Well, I brought your tray."

"Thank you." She straightened out her clothes, best she could. "Do you ever think about freedom?"

Lucy cocked her head as if it were a trick question. "You mean like for the colonies?"

"Well, yes. The colonies or your own freedom or both."

"I don't know. We talk about getting papers so's we can be free. I wish my James, my little boy, had been born a free man. It's not so bad here in Boston—here with the Wheatleys—but there's never no telling. We could get sold off should anything happen. Get sold down South and all separated."

"I guess I don't think that much about being sold." Phillis wondered how many other things she had never considered.

Lucy clucked her tongue. "No. I'm thinking you wouldn't have worried 'bout that." She opened the door and left without another word.

Phillis sighed and prayed. *Lord, help me watch my tongue. I want to build a bridge to Lucy, not say words that remind her of the gulf between us.*

Plans for Mary's wedding filled many a day. Phillis was happy to help and even penned invitations to the wedding supper. Mrs. Wheatley talked with Sadie at length about food.

"Because the wedding will be in winter, let's have something warm and heartening. Perhaps a New England boiled supper, apple tansy, and finish the meal with Dutch cheese, then a dish of coffee."

Mary spent so much time preparing her linens and the things she would need to set up a new household that she didn't worry much about the marriage ceremony or supper. She worried most about being a good minister's wife.

But all the while they worked on preparations, Phillis noticed a new weariness in Mrs. Wheatley. Her mistress—the woman who had become like a mother to her—was getting on in years. She'd be sixty-two on her next birthday.

"Mrs. Wheatley, why don't you sit down and let me pin that bodice on Mary."

"She's right, Mother. You sit and we'll work."

"But Phillis should be upstairs writing." Mrs. Wheatley lowered herself into a chair as she spoke. "I don't want to take her away from her work."

"I need a break from my writing every now and then. Surely you don't want my eyes to get squinty and my shoulders crabbed from too many hours huddled over my writing."

Mary laughed. "Methinks you're playing it a bit dramatic, dear student."

They all laughed at Phillis's expense, but laughter and work made for a merry late summer afternoon.

As Phillis watched Mary and her mother she couldn't help thinking back to her own mother. Was she well? The brothers would be considered men now, living in their own huts. She wondered what kind of men they were. She was sure that like all young men they would continue to take care of their mother. Did *Maamanding* still think of her? Did she have any idea her Janxa lived?

Phillis hadn't thought of that name in a very long time. Janxa. That girl felt like another person. Had Phillis ever walked through elephant grass listening to the chattering of monkeys?

Did the same *griot* come through the village, or was it his son now? Did they sing of her and her father? Even after this time? She wondered what the *griot* would say if he could see her poems, written on paper or published in a newspaper.

"Phillis, you are woolgathering again," Mary said. "If you stick any more pins in me, I don't think I shall ever get out of this bodice."

"Well, that may be a good way of keeping you here," Phillis said. Until she spoke the words, she hadn't realized how much she dreaded losing Mary. Nathaniel already spent most of his time away. He'd bought out much of his father's business interests, and he kept busy trading between Boston and London, sailing on the family ship.

"I believe if you tried to keep me here, my John would come to rescue me."

They all laughed, but Phillis couldn't get rid of the feeling that things were changing way too fast. The riot last spring—the one they now called the Boston Massacre— seemed to usher in a new era of tension. With so many tariffs and taxes, boycotts and embargoes, Boston was a different city than the one in which she landed. And now, with all this talk of freedom, she couldn't help thinking about her own place in this world.

She loved the Wheatleys—especially Mary and Mrs. Wheatley. They had treated her like a daughter of the house. And Mrs. Wheatley was still determined to see Phillis published. She used the word *book* more and more lately. It sent chills down Phillis's spine.

But despite all that, she was still a slave. She wondered if Mr. Wheatley ever considered manumission papers, making her free? Perhaps she should ask. She was stuck in that uncomfortable spot her master talked about when he referred to something as "neither fish nor fowl."

As her master and mistress got older, anything could happen. She was still a slave, even though they didn't call her that. In most homes in Boston, slaves were called "servants for life." The terms didn't change anything, though. They were still property. She would be noted as chattel in their last will and testament one day. Who could say she wouldn't be sold then? Even sold down South.

Things were changing. And Phillis's hunger for freedom grew much like the fledgling colonies' fight for freedom.

An Elegy of Hope

Boston, 1770

"Oh, Sadie." Phillis went into the kitchen. "Mrs. Wheatley says to tell you we're having company this evening."

Sadie shook her head. "How many this time?"

"It's to be twelve, but that's not the news." Phillis was now about seventeen years old, and she'd been used to Wheatley dinner parties for almost ten years.

Sadie opened the larder to see what she would cook. "What news?"

"The dinner party is for Reverend George Whitefield." Phillis clasped her hands together. "Can you believe it?"

"Lands above." Sadie stopped taking inventory. "Reverend Whitefield is in America and will be eatin' my cookin' tonight?" She sat down. "I can remember the first time I heard him preach. It was a sight to behold."

"I know. I'd heard he could preach to tens of thousands,

but I didn't believe it at first. How could any man's voice be heard by so many?" Phillis shook her head. "Our own Benjamin Franklin didn't credit it, but when he heard him in Philadelphia he wrote that he couldn't believe the reverend's powerful voice. Mr. Franklin moved away from the reverend's voice until he could only faintly hear the preaching and then he estimated the distance. He said if you figured two square feet per person, Reverend Whitefield had easily spoken to tens of thousands."

"He loves preaching to Negroes and working folk. It's why he's so admired." Sadie stood up. "I need to be gettin' that fine ham I have down in the cellar. I been saving it for something special."

"Mrs. Wheatley has been working with the Countess of Huntington to raise funds for the orphanage Reverend Whitefield started all those years ago in Georgia." Phillis laughed. "If I know her, she'll ask me to read my most poignant poem tonight to help squeeze as many purses as we can."

"Uh oh!" Sadie stopped.

"What?"

"I'm going to have to cook and wait tables tonight."

"Why? Where's Lucy?" Ever since Phillis had begun praying for Lucy she'd been more aware of her than ever. Each time she saw her, she prayed. She didn't know what God was doing in Lucy's life, but even if those prayers hadn't touched Lucy, they'd changed Phillis over the last two years.

"Her baby boy is bad sick. Lucy's beside herself. I told her to take time off so's she can just hold the little James."

"I'll help you wait table." Phillis didn't mind at all.

"I can't have you do that. What will the Missus say?"

"I'll tell her myself." Phillis knew she wouldn't mind. As the years had passed, Mrs. Wheatley cared less about the way things appeared. The thing she fervently cared about was spreading the gospel and squeezing every last coin she could finagle out of her friends and acquaintances to do that.

That night, as Phillis began the dinner service, Mr. Wheatley introduced her to the guests. "You've all heard about our famous poet, Phillis Wheatley. I'd like to introduce her." He proceeded to introduce her to everyone seated at the table.

Phillis could see that some of the guests were uncomfortable. They didn't know how to treat her—as a fellow diner or as a servant. Phillis wanted to put them at ease. "I'm helping with service tonight because Lucy, who usually serves, has a very sick child."

Mrs. Wheatley smiled. "Phillis is one of the family, and she's always been there for us in a pinch."

"I like that about you, young lady," Reverend Whitefield said. "Not many people know this, but when I was a student, I was so poor I had to start Oxford as a servitor." He turned to Phillis. "That meant that I received free tuition in exchange for acting as personal servant to three other wealthy students."

There were whispers of surprise around the table.

"I didn't have a father—only my mother, an innkeeper. Perhaps that's one of the reasons I started my orphanage. I did not grow up the son of privilege."

Mrs. Wheatley began to speak about the orphanage. When Phillis had cleared the soup bowls and served the main course, the table still heard stories of children whose lives were changed at Bethesda Orphanage. She couldn't help smiling as she looked around the table. There would be many more orphanage benefactors after tonight.

As Phillis finished service, Mrs. Wheatley asked her to sit down with them. Phillis could hear Reverend Whitefield wheezing. She recognized it as the asthma.

"Would you like a glass of cool water, Reverend Whitefield?" she asked.

"I would, indeed. I'm guessing you are a fellow asthma sufferer to recognize it in me."

She smiled her answer and went to get a glass of cool well water. Sometimes when the tightness came, she could relieve some of it by sipping cool water. Or maybe it only helped relax her.

As she went into the kitchen, she saw Sadie sitting by the stove with her hands pressing the skirt of her apron to her face.

"Sadie, what's wrong?"

Sadie's body convulsed with sobs. "Lucy's child died tonight. He went home to be with the Lord." She rocked back and forth. "He was just a little bit of a thing—Lucy's only child."

"Let me take this water, and I'll be right back."

She handed the water to Reverend Whitefield, excused herself, and motioned for Mrs. Wheatley to follow. In the butler's pantry, she told her mistress the sad news and asked to be excused from reading and reciting for the evening.

"Certainly, child. We will stop and ask prayer for them. You run along." As she started back to the dining room, she turned around and said, "Thank you for tonight."

As Phillis went back into the kitchen, she put on a bigger apron. "I want to help you clean up tonight."

"No," Sadie said. "I'll get myself together. Jus' give me a minute."

"Why don't you take plates of food for Lucy and her husband and sit with them a while? You are like a mother to Lucy."

Sadie looked around the kitchen.

"I can clean this up while I pray for Lucy. You go." Phillis began cutting slices of ham and putting together plates of food, while Sadie washed her face and put on a clean apron.

"Thank you, child," Sadie said as she put a hand on Phillis's cheek.

Phillis waited until the last carriage left to begin to clear off the table.

Prince came in to lend a hand, removing his frock coat. "Sadie asked me to help you out here." He finished clearing the table and setting the dining room to rights. Phillis did the dishes, and he fetched water. It felt good to work hard.

By the time she got to her room she was bone tired but keyed up. So many things went through her mind. What a night. She would never forget that she met Reverend George Whitefield and found out he, too, came from humble beginnings. She loved the stories they told of the revival they called the Great Awakening. She watched this man afflicted by lung ailments and yet working as hard as ever. As he told them tonight, "I'd rather wear out than rust out."

But then the sad news of Lucy's little James. Praying for Lucy had become a habit with Phillis, but tonight, she prayed with new urgency. *Lord, comfort them. Let them see things from an eternal viewpoint.*

She sat down at the desk, took out a fresh piece of paper, and opened her inkwell. Of all the poems she wrote, she loved writing elegies the best. Mary never did understand it.

"Why do you spend so much time writing about those who've died?" she would ask.

Phillis never did explain it. How could she? How did you explain what you learned from a dead gazelle calf hanging from a tree or people being thrown off a slave ship because illness was suspected? Perhaps it had to do with losing your father, mother, and brothers when you were only seven years old. Whatever it was, Phillis had learned to see death as a gateway.

She didn't believe death was final. The Bible spoke clearly on that. Nothing made sense in life until you understood that. Death was the gateway to eternal life. As soon as Phillis heard about a death in her church or among their friends, she longed to comfort the survivors by trying to give them a glimpse of their loved one in eternity.

Tonight was no different. She began to write:

The blooming babe, with shades of death o'erspread,
No more shall smile, no more shall raise its head,
But like a branch that from the tree is torn,
Fall prostrate, wither'd, languid, and forlorn.

She put her pen down and blotted her words. She didn't know if Lucy would accept her words. If only she'd be comforted. She dipped her pen again and kept writing:

"Where flies my James?" 'tis thus I seem to hear
The parents ask, "Some angel tell me where
He wings his passage through the yielding air?"
Methinks a cherub bending from the skies
Observes the question, and serene replies,
"In heav'ns high places your babe appears:
Prepare to meet him, and dismiss your tears."

Phillis kept writing long into the night. When she finally finished the elegy she recopied it, blotted it, folded it, and tied it with a black ribbon.

Morning came too soon. Phillis woke with a tapping on the door. "Come in."

Lucy came in with a breakfast tray. Her eyes were swollen and she shuffled as she moved.

"I did not expect you this day," Phillis said. *What a thoughtless thing to say,* she thought. *Lord, help me.*

"I didn't know what else to do with myself."

"Lucy . . . I'm so sorry. I'm—"

"Sadie told me you served last night and cleaned up so she could be with me." Lucy folded her hands. Her head hung. "I wanted to say my thanks."

Phillis went over to the desk to get the elegy. "I wrote a poem for your James last night." She held it out, but Lucy didn't take it.

"For my baby? You wrote a poem for our James?" Lucy sat down hard in the chair near the bed. "No one ever wrote a poem for a slave baby before, did they?"

"I don't know. I didn't think of him that way."

Lucy was quiet for a long time. "Will you read it to me? I can't read."

Phillis untied the ribbon and began to read. As she read, the tears ran down Lucy's face, but she didn't make a sound.

When she finished, Lucy asked, "Read the line about heaven's high places again."

Phillis read: "In heav'ns high places your babe appears: Prepare to meet him, and dismiss your tears."

"It is the most beautiful poem I ever heard." She took a handkerchief out of her pocket and blotted the tears on her face and blew her nose. "This morning I woke up not knowing how I could live without my little boy. Now I know. We need to prepare to meet him."

Phillis tied the ribbon around the poem.

"Will you tell me what I need to do to make sure I'll be with James in heaven someday?"

When Lucy left the room a while later, Phillis knew her prayers had been answered—not in the way she would have chosen, but she wasn't about to start questioning God about why He did the things He did. Once you started that, you could keep going in circles forever.

Why did God let James die? Why did God let *tubaab* capture her father and her? Why did her new country have to continue to struggle for the tiniest bit of freedom? Why did she still live as a slave, when she yearned for freedom?

She could let those questions rule her life if she fixed on them.

As she had come to know God, she discovered His love for her. Just as she always trusted her own father without questioning his actions, she needed to trust her heavenly Father.

After nine years in the Wheatley house, she finally had a friend in Lucy.

~⁂~   ~⁂~   ~⁂~   ~⁂~

It was barely a fortnight after she read the elegy for Lucy's son at his funeral that she had to begin another.

As she came into the library one morning, she found Mrs. Wheatley holding a letter and crying. "The Reverend Whitefield died."

"But he was just here." Despite his asthma, Phillis could sense his vitality.

"He preached to a huge crowd in a field. He stood atop a barrel to be seen." She wiped her eyes with the tip of her hankie. "The next morning he died. It was his lungs."

"What a loss for us, but what joy there must be in heaven." Phillis knew she needed to find pen and paper.

She spent the next days at her desk working on the elegy for this man she admired. When she finally finished it, she brought it down to Mrs. Wheatley and went to take a walk in the garden. How good it was for her grief to work it out on paper.

When she came back inside, Mrs. Wheatley sat at her desk with the poem. "Can you make two more copies of the elegy?"

"Yes. I shall do it now."

"I want to send it to the Countess of Huntingdon in London. Reverend Whitefield was her chaplain. Mr. Wheatley's ship sails tomorrow, so I'd like to have it ready."

Phillis prepared the copies and gave them to Mrs. Wheatley. The act of writing the poem was her gift to the memory of a man she would never forget.

Freedom
at Last

Boston, 1771

"Phillis!" Mrs. Wheatley's voice had carried from the vestibule all the way to the attic.

Phillis came running down the stairs. Mrs. Wheatley never shouted. In all the years Phillis had lived in the house, if she were needed, her mistress would send someone upstairs to summon her.

Her heart thudded as she cleared the last step. "Are you ill?"

"No, child. I didn't mean to alarm you; it's just that I have the most interesting news." She held out a letter and waved it in the air like a flag. "This is from Selina Hastings, the Countess of Huntingdon, the London believer who worked on behalf of her chaplain, Reverend Whitefield."

"Yes, I remember you telling me about her." Phillis wished Mrs. Wheatley would get to the news. She so easily became distracted these days.

"When you copied the elegy you wrote for Reverend Whitefield, I sent one copy to the Countess and another to William Legge, the Earl of Dartmouth."

Phillis hadn't thought about the poem since the day she wrote it.

"The Countess writes that your elegy has been published as a broadside and is being read by everyone in England." She emphasized the word *everyone*. "She says all of England is talking about you."

Everyone? Phillis had to go into the parlor and sit down. Mrs. Wheatley followed.

"She says that it is to be published and distributed here in the colonies as well."

"I hardly know what to say." Phillis was not often at a loss for words.

"Here is what we shall do . . ." Phillis recognized Mrs. Wheatley's tactical voice. Phillis and Mary used to laugh when she began to formulate plans. She hardly stopped to breathe. "You collect and polish your very best poems. We will take out an advertisement in the *Boston Censor* for a subscription to your book—*Poems on Various Subjects*." Mrs. Wheatley clasped her hands together. "As soon as we have enough subscribers, we'll have it printed and bound."

"But with all the trouble and taxes here in Boston, will anyone want to buy a book of poetry?" Phillis asked.

"We won't know unless we try." She tapped her hand against her mouth, looking up to the ceiling before she spoke again. "I shall write the Countess and Dartmouth as well about a possible British edition." She stood up. "Let's get to work. You work on compiling the poems; I shall write advertisements and letters."

Phillis started work on her collected poems that day.

Boston, 1772

Phillis stood in the kitchen, watching Sadie and Lucy sorting squash and pumpkins picked from the garden. They'd be cooking the blemished ones and taking the others into the root cellar to pack down in straw so they would last into the winter months. Phillis hoped Sadie's pumpkin soup would be on tonight's menu. Not that she expected to have much appetite.

"So tell us again, child, what is it you have to do?" Sadie used that voice she saved for things that didn't make any sense to her.

"There's some that just don't credit a slave could be writing the things our Phillis writes," Lucy said, answering for Phillis.

Phillis nodded. "Lucy's right. There's too much at stake here. I've been called to prove myself before a panel of America's harshest critics."

"How do you do that? Will you sit yourself down in plain sight of all those wig-wearing nabobs and make some poems?" When Sadie stood there, hands on hips and feet solidly planted on the kitchen floor, Phillis recognized her don't-be-messin'-with-me look.

"I don't really know. I think I am to stand before them

and they will ask me questions." Just the thought of it made her heart beat in her throat. The idea of standing in front of all those distinguished men made her twitch. Her chest felt tight.

The next morning she still fidgeted, standing first on one foot and then on the other, as Prince brought the carriage around for the short ride to her interrogation. Who would have thought she'd have to prove that she wrote the poems herself? Did Milton have to prove his authorship? What about Alexander Pope? Shakespeare?

She carried the pages on which she had copied the twenty poems she'd polished for her proposed book. Mr. Wheatley helped her into the carriage and then climbed in to sit beside her. She was glad he would accompany her. "You shall do just fine, Phillis. You'll answer their questions, and they'll sign an attestation that the poems were, in truth, written only by you."

"So my word is not enough?" Phillis didn't meant to sound cranky. It was just that she was nervous.

"Phillis, you are a slave. Most people do not believe a slave can even be taught to read, let alone become a celebrated poet. Think, girl, how many women here in the colonies have been published, let alone a slave girl."

Phillis hated being reminded she remained a slave. But if she had to be tested by a panel of powerful men, so be it. She shifted the sheaf of papers in her hands so the pages would not become damp from perspiration.

"Welcome, Phillis, Mr. Wheatley. Please be seated." His Excellency, Thomas Hutchinson, governor of Massachusetts, presided.

Phillis looked around the room. She recognized them all. There were several ministers, many statesmen—both loyalists and patriots. She nodded to John Hancock and the Reverend Samuel Cooper, the minister who had baptized her.

Before she had time to get her bearings, they started the questioning. Once she could see the line of questioning, she relaxed some. They asked questions about her studies. Who was Calliope? Could she name the other muses? What was iambic pentameter? What poets had she read?

At first she could sense skepticism, but as she answered question after question, she sensed a new respect around the room. She found herself enjoying the examination. She wondered if this is what it would have been like had she been able to have a formal education.

By the time it was over, she had an affidavit, signed by all eighteen men, attesting that she was the author of the collection. They agreed that a slave had indeed written the poems.

Boston, 1774

Phillis felt the smooth wood of the ship's railing as it made the wide turn into Boston Harbor. So much had happened since the day of that examination. It wouldn't be the last time someone questioned whether or not a slave girl could have written a poem, let alone a published book of poems. But she had. And in a short time, she'd have that leather-covered book in her hands.

"Is this your first time sailing into Boston, ma'am?" a sailor asked her.

"No, but this time it feels as if I'm coming home."

It was thirteen years ago a frightened, half-starved African child sailed into Boston harbor aboard that reeking slave ship—a ship of death.

Not long after that day she saw Susanna Wheatley for the first time. The woman she'd come to love like a mother. Now Phillis was coming back to Boston because Mrs. Wheatley needed her.

She couldn't help reminiscing. What was it about a sea voyage that gave one space to think about the whole of life?

Ever since she could remember, she'd longed to be a storyteller. In Africa, she dreamed of becoming a *griot*, but it wasn't until she came to America that she discovered written language. How she fell in love with words!

The Lord knew all along what He had in store for her— from that first longing to create a song for a gazelle. She took one small step after another—first learning to read and write, then getting a poem published, and then one poem after another. Each step was part of God's plan.

The ship's bell rang and brought Phillis back to the present. For now, she needed to disembark and make her way to the Wheatley house on King Street. It had been a full two months since she received the letter in England telling her Susanna Wheatley was gravely ill and needed her. Phillis had been praying the whole voyage that she'd find her mistress still living. She wanted the chance to care for Mrs. Wheatley now.

As she came off the ship—very near where she landed the first time she came to Boston—Prince waited with the carriage.

"Welcome home, Phillis. Welcome home. Let me get your trunk." He hurried off to the place where the sailors unloaded the luggage.

Phillis looked at the seat cushions and rubbed her hand across the smooth leather. She remembered hearing her name for the first time in this very carriage, and taking her finger and marking out the letters P H I L L I S.

"I stowed your luggage," Prince said, climbing into the driver's seat. "It's a shame your time in London was cut short, but I'm glad you're back. The Missus kept asking for you."

"I'm glad I'm back as well."

"Did you get your books?"

"No, I had to return before they finished printing them. They should follow soon." Phillis couldn't believe her book was being published. So far the American version hadn't sold, but soon she'd have the British version.

"Is Nathaniel well?" Prince asked. He had been with the family since Nathaniel and Mary were toddlers.

"Yes, he's well and happy. I left him in London." The carriage bumped over the cobbles. "I'm beginning to think he won't be coming back to America to live. I think he'll run the business from London."

"You don't think he wants to be an American?"

Phillis didn't know for sure, but she didn't sense that passion in him for this new country. "I don't think so."

"Miss Mary and her preacher husband, they are patriots. I hope they keep themselves out of trouble with the British."

"How is Mary?"

Prince paused. "I think she's troubled with illness much of the time, but to hear her tell, you wouldn't know it."

They pulled up in front of the house. Sadie and Lucy came out to greet her.

"Land, child. You look mighty good. We been missing you around here." Sadie put arms around her and squeezed. "Um, um, um, you didn't add much meat to those bones."

Lucy stepped up and gave Phillis a kiss. "I prayed every day that God would keep you safe."

"I'm so glad to be home." How good that word sounded. Home. "How is Mrs. Wheatley?"

"She's weak, but she keeps on asking for you. The closer the time came for your homecoming, the more she perked up." Sadie laughed. "I don't think she'd dare miss getting that book of yours."

"Besides," Lucy said, "she wants to hear 'bout everything you did. Don't be thinkin' you can leave anything out of the telling."

Phillis thanked Prince for driving her. As she walked into the house, she felt that peace of belonging. Yes, she was home. She headed straight up to Mrs. Wheatley's room with Lucy and Sadie trailing.

"You are home!"

"I am." Her mistress looked weak. When had she gotten so old?

"Lucy, will you bring tea and something to eat? I know the child is hungry, but I want to hear everything." Mrs. Wheatley struggled to sit up. Sadie propped pillows behind her. "I hated to send for you before you had a chance to meet everyone and see the book all the way through the printing, but how I longed for you to be here."

"When I heard you needed me, I was only too glad to come home." Phillis smiled at Sadie as the cook silently took her leave.

"We originally sent you to London for your health. Did the sea air help?"

Phillis rubbed her chest absently. "I don't know if it did or not. I just know I'm happiest here at home."

"Did you meet the Countess?"

"No. I didn't have the opportunity. She'd gone to her home in Wales." Phillis could sense Mrs. Wheatley's disappointment. "But I did meet ever so many others, including Benjamin Franklin."

"So even though you were only there a few weeks, you had a good visit?"

"I was the toast of the town." Phillis laughed. "Can you imagine the consternation—a slave, an African, and a celebrated American poet? England didn't know what to do with me."

"Ah, yes . . . a slave." Mrs. Wheatley reached toward a small box on the table next to her bed and took out an envelope. "About that . . . Mr. Wheatley helped me draw these up. It's for you." She handed the packet to Phillis.

Phillis opened the envelope and took out the documents. She stopped at the first page and looked at Mrs. Wheatley. She didn't know what to say. They were her manumission papers. She was a slave no longer. The papers declared her a free woman.

"It doesn't mean you're not still part of the family," Mrs.

Wheatley said in a soft voice. "This is your home. But as we watched the people of Boston struggle for freedom, I began to understand how precious it is. I don't know why it took so long to realize that tyranny and slavery weren't so very different. As we've watched the colonies struggle toward freedom from oppression, I recognized that you must also long for freedom from slavery."

It was as Phillis had once written to Lord Dartmouth:

> Should you my lord, while you peruse my song,
> Wonder from whence my love of Freedom sprung,
> Whence flow these wishes for the common good,
> By feeling hearts alone best understood,
> I, young in life, by seeming cruel fate
> Was snatch'd from Afric's fancy'd happy seat:
> What pangs excruciating must molest,
> What sorrows labour in my parent's breast?
> Steel'd was that soul and by no misery mov'd
> That from a father seiz'd his babe belov'd:
> Such, such my case. And can I then but pray
> Others may never feel tyrannic sway?

Her journey from Africa to America had been a painful one, but she could see God's hand in all of it. In her new country she'd found freedom. The freedom of the *griot* that came from telling stories, freedom from slavery, and the greatest freedom of all—freedom in Christ.

Phillis couldn't speak. She put her arms around the now frail woman and whispered, "Thank you."

Notes on Phillis Wheatley

Through the years, readers have longed to know what Phillis Wheatley's life was like before she was kidnapped into slavery. Sadly, Phillis only mentioned Africa three times in her writings and letters, including the memory of her mother pouring out water before the sun and of being snatched from her father's arms. Because she never said what her name had been in Africa, I chose the word *janxa* to use as her name. The word simply means "girl" in Wolof, which was probably her native tongue. It would not have been her name, but because naming is so important in her culture, the story could not have been told without giving her a name.

We do not know about Phillis's siblings or the exact village she came from, but she did write that she came from Gambia, which would mean from the region we now call Senegambia.

We do know the exact slave ship she boarded, the owner of that ship, and its captain. We're not certain who came with her—some speculate that Obour sailed with her to Boston; others think she met Obour in Newport. But Obour Tanner was real and, after Phillis grew up, Obour acted as a literary agent of sorts to Phillis.

We don't know anything about the Wheatleys' cook or housekeeper, so Sadie and Lucy are both fictional characters. The poem I had Phillis write for Lucy's son was an actual elegy written by Phillis, though probably not for someone in their household.

Phillis's life in Boston, from the auction block to her untimely death at the age of about thirty, is well documented.

I tell her story to the day she realizes her dream of freedom. There's more to the story, however. It's ground covered in other books. After Susanna Wheatley died, Phillis lived for a time with Mary and her husband, while the new nation was in chaos, fighting for its own freedom. When John Wheatley died, he failed to remember Phillis in his will. Perhaps Susanna and John Wheatley believed that along with Phillis's fame would come wealth, or perhaps they just followed the custom of the day, settling the inheritance on the oldest son. Whatever the reason, everything went to Nathaniel, who ended up making his home in England.

Phillis continued to support herself with her writing, but in this struggling new nation, it was not easy for a poet to make a living. She eventually married a free man, John Peters, and had three children, all of whom died as babies. Phillis's health troubled her to the end. She died young, but we know that, as she wrote in so many of her elegies, she believed death to be the ultimate triumph.

Over the years there has been much controversy about

Phillis Wheatley. In her day, she had to prove over and over that a slave could write sophisticated, classically inspired poetry. In the mid to late twentieth century, many criticized her poetry for being "too white." Critics wondered why she abandoned all the experiences of a childhood in Africa and as a slave to create religious verse with European sensibilities.

Scholars today are rediscovering Phillis Wheatley. As Henry Louis Gates Jr. said in the 2002 Jefferson Lecture in the Humanities at the Library of Congress, "And even now, so the imperative remains: to cast aside the mine-and-thine rhetoric of cultural ownership. For cultures can be no more owned than people can. . . . And so we're reminded of our task: to learn to read Wheatley anew, unblinkered by the anxieties of her time and ours. . . . The challenge isn't to read white, or read black; it is to read."[1]

NOTE
1. Henry Louis Gates Jr., *The Trials of Phillis Wheatley* (New York: Basic Civitas Books, 2003), 85, 89.

Glossary

Allah: the Muslim deity
baobab: an African tree known for its thick trunk
chattel: property; a slave with no right to freedom
couscous: pasta made from millet
griot: a storyteller in Africa, usually one who travels from one village to another
kora: a stringed African instrument
Maamanding: Mother
maize: corn
manumission: officially freeing a slave
mbubba: an African dress consisting of cloth wrapped around the body
tama: a form of African drum
tubaab: white people

DAUGHTERS OF THE FAITH

Young Harriet Tubman grew up in the early 1800's as a slave in Maryland. The story of her childhood is the story of God's faithfulness as He prepares her to eventually lead more than 300 people out of slavery through the Underground Railroad.

ISBN-13: 978-0-8024-4098-3

Olice Oatman and her sister are captured when their wagon train is raded by outlaw Yavapais. After enduring harsh treatment, they are ransomed by a band of Mohaves. She learns to see the Mohave design tattooed on her chin as a sign of God's love and deliverance.

ISBN-13: 978-0-8024-3638-2

In 1761 Phillis Wheatley was captured in Gambia and brought to America as a slave. She became the first African American to publish a book, and her writings would eventually win her freedom. But more importantly, her poetry still proclaims Christ.

ISBN-13: 978-0-8024-7639-5

A fascinating true-life story of 16-year-old Eliza Shirley who traveled from England to the United States to pioneer the work of the Salvation Army.

ISBN-13: 978-0-8024-4073-0

MOODY
PUBLISHERS.

1-800-678-8812 · MOODYPUBLISHERS.COM

MORE DAUGHTERS OF THE FAITH

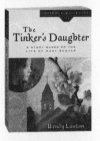